ADVANCE PRAISE FOR ELORA OF STONE

"[Jaime Lee Mann] captured a little bit of everything that's been really popular and intriguing for these readers."

- Karen Mair, CBC's *Mainstreet PEI* radio show

"This was an interesting fantasy read... It's fast paced, entertaining, and I found myself worrying about the two main characters."

- Jo Ann Hakola, aka The Book Faerie, *Journey of a Bookseller* review blog

"I love the central plot in this book. It's a great world with some interesting characters and solid plot twists... a solid start to a series and likely to go over well with young

fans of fantasy."

   - Martha Dodge, *The One and Only Marfalfa* review blog

"This is a magical book of spells and goblins... From the opening page, the descriptions are so vivid!"

   - Paul Alan, *House of Q* radio show

"Who knew you could throw so many curves into one hundred and fifty pages. This thrilling ride of sorcery and magic had the students in my class fully enveloped! I would recommend it to everyone, whether you are a grade four student or a grade four teacher!"

   - Eric VanWiechen, grade four teacher, Morell Consolidated School

"*Elora of Stone* is nothing like any other book I've ever read, I love it."

   - Trysten, grade four student

"I really want to buy [*Elora of Stone*] whenever it comes out and never stop reading it."

   - Jacob, grade four student

ELORA OF STONE

The "Legend of Rhyme" Series Volume 1 Book 1

By Jaime Lee Mann

To Casey and Shelby.

I love you so much, I'd eat you for lunch.

CONTENTS

INTRODUCTION

As a little girl, I adored my dad's made-up stories. Being read to was wonderful, of course, but I just loved getting lost in Dad's silly tales about the white horse that could never stay clean, the crazy old sandman, or the two little girls who couldn't find their way out of the woods.

Dad might not realize it (until he reads this!), but I've carried his stories in my heart throughout my whole life. They're a very cherished part of my childhood.

When I became a mother, my husband and I found ourselves with two little girls who did not like sleeping. I took a lesson from my dad and started making up stories that would go on and on, until the sound of my voice eventually put the children to sleep.

There was one particular story, though, that did not send the girls to dreamland. Quite the opposite, actually. This one story—about a little girl, an enchanted tree, and a magical land—had my daughters buzzing with excitement and begging to hear more, night after night.

They asked to hear the story so often, that I thought I should write it down.

That little bedtime story was the beginning of the Legend of Rhyme series. I hope you enjoy Elora of Stone as much as my daughters do.

By the way, these days, the girls are much better sleepers, but they still haven't gotten tired of hearing my stories before bed. It's probably safe to assume that most of the stories you read by me were inspired on the floor of my little girls' bedroom. I'm not quite sure what I'll write about when they grow up, as children tend to do, but I'm sure I'll think of something.

MAP OF RHYME

Island of Rhyme

Village

Statue of Edara

Poison Ivy

Pine Tree

Grumblcroot's
Underground Lair

Casius' Hut

N
W E
S

100 FEET ABOVE SEA LEVEL

Once upon a full moon…

CHAPTER ONE

Snatched

GRIMBLEROD REACHES one grimy green hand up into the thin white roots of the plants above. His other hand steadies the candle near eye level. The roots twist in knots, curling into each other, clinging to the dirt like tiny gnarled fists. Grimblerod pinches two long dirty fingers around a juicy grub.

Bringing his fingers to his face, Grimblerod studies the grub more closely in the candlelight. Satisfied with his prize, he pulls a leather drawstring pouch from the pocket of his tattered trousers and plops the grub inside.

Grimblerod's stomach twists with hunger, but he has work to do. His candle is close to burning out, and beads of melted wax drip onto his hand, leaving bumpy yellow trails along his skin. He has just enough light to get to the opening in the tree.

He grunts as he trudges along, piercing the deafening silence with snorts and other impolite sounds. Once he reaches the opening, Grimblerod blows out his candle and sets it down. He then shimmies his fat little body up a slender brown root into the fresh night air.

After clawing his way up to the surface, Grimblerod shields his eyes against the light of the full moon. Instinctively, he checks his feet, and, seeing that he is still in goblin form, he nods to the sky.

The sound of crickets drowns out his rumbling stomach, and the glow of the moon guides him through the dark.

A thick, white mist creeps along, hiding him from sight. A gentle breeze rustles the leaves on the giant tree making them tremble in the night.

An owl cries out in the dark. One might say it was warning the villagers of the evil acts about to occur.

It is the type of setting the worst dreams start with,

and tonight, a mother's most unspeakable nightmare will come true.

Before he takes another step, Grimblerod must eat. He pulls the grub from his pouch and places it between his sharp pointy teeth. He bites down on the creature, filling his mouth with yellow and green liquid.

As he chews, he reaches into his pouch again, this time for a smooth green stone. He holds it to his head and closes his eyes.

He hears his master's voice. *Grimblerod, tonight there are three for you to take, while the moon is full.*

He rubs the stone on his head and sees a basic hut with a thatched roof standing in the middle of a wide open field. As the vision becomes clearer, he snaps his fingers, and the stone transports him inside the very hut he has pictured.

Two little babies sleep peacefully on a straw mat between their parents.

Grimblerod quietly creeps across the cold dirt floor.

Reaching again into his leather pouch, he pulls out a

small wooden doll. He takes the stone from his hand and rubs it over the doll, transforming the object into an exact replica of the sleeping baby he is about to take. Except the replica will never breathe.

Grimblerod's thin black lips curve into a smile as his short little body carefully lifts the sleeping baby. He gingerly places the enchanted doll in its place, and puts the stone to his head once more. He is transported to the pixie tree, where he leaves the chubby pink baby in an enchanted glass box.

The smiling baby kicks its legs inside its nightgown. As Grimblerod waddles away from the tree, the box vanishes, along with its contents.

Again, Grimblerod places the green stone to his forehead. He sees the next dwelling he must visit tonight. This time, he must go within the stone walls of the castle, on the island of Valorium. The wealthy are not immune to Larque's heartless work.

Over the years, Grimblerod's master Larque has sent him for hundreds of babies. What happens to the infants after he leaves them here in this glass box, Grimblerod does not know, but he does know better than to ask.

If goblins were capable of caring about human feelings, Grimblerod would have questioned the motives of his master at some point along the way. He may even have wondered if the children ever had the chance to grow up.

Grimblerod doesn't care that the next day when the parents wake, they will believe their babies have died in the night. The dolls will be buried, the babies mourned.

CHAPTER TWO

Before Our Story Begins

SIX-YEAR-OLD GWENDOLYN Celli skips along the old logging path ahead of her parents, Anna and Ivan. Leaves crunch beneath her feet.

A soft breeze rustles the crisp orange, red, and yellow leaves on the trees. Patches of blue peek through the forest's autumn canopy. The way the light shines in through the gold and brown leaves, it looks to Gwendolyn that the forest is glowing from within.

Gwendolyn stops every few steps, watching the leaves lazily float to the ground. She squeals with delight each time one lands in her outstretched hands. Her enthusiasm over such simple things makes her nervous mother smile.

"Don't you get too far ahead of us, Gwendolyn!" Anna calls to her daughter.

"I won't! I know how to not get lost!"

Anna walks with her husband behind this miniature replica of herself. While Gwendolyn and her father share the same twinkling blue eyes, the girl has her mother's fine features and chestnut brown hair. They even share the same trail of freckles across the bridge of their noses. But, while Anna's hair hangs in soft waves around her face, Gwendolyn's is a mess of long wild curls.

"Are you sure about this, Ivan?" Anna asks, taking his hand. Her rose-coloured lips tighten into a concerned thin line.

"Rebecca Caine is a wise woman, Anna," Ivan says. "If she believes it is our destiny to marry our Gwendolyn to her Lochlan, well... I trust her."

The look on Ivan's face suggests to Anna that he may feel otherwise.

A twig snaps loudly, breaking under Gwendolyn's feet.

Startled, Anna drops Ivan's hand.

"Slow down, love!" she calls after her daughter. "Be careful you don't trip and soil your good dress!"

Anna turns to Ivan. "Are we sure this is what we want for our daughter? To make the decision now about who she is to marry, while she is still a little girl?"

"This is how things are done, Anna. I'm surprised you would say such a thing," Ivan replies.

"Just because this is the way it has always been done, must we do the same?"

"We will see what Rebecca has to say," Ivan says. "And decide from there."

"Aren't you worried about marrying her into a family of witches?" asks Anna.

"The Caines are good witches, Anna. Rebecca is a descendant of Elora, The Good. I don't believe Gwendolyn will be in any danger."

Anna takes a deep breath. The crisp autumn air smells musty, like earth, moss, and decaying leaves. Death making way for new life. This is how the forest works.

The smell of fall in the air always brings her back to that day six years ago. The morning after Gwendolyn and her sister were born. The morning only one tiny twin awoke.

Pushing that sad memory down inside, she takes her husband's hand again and says, "I suppose it can't hurt to talk to her."

"If we don't like what she has to say, Anna, we will leave."

Anna nods.

Up ahead, Gwendolyn is enthralled with the patterns of light the sun tosses through the trees and how it dances in fluid shapes on the lush forest carpet.

A pair of chipmunks scurry down from a nearby tree and sit beside the child.

"Ivan, do you see that?" Anna puts her arm out to stop him from walking any farther.

A skinny, beige rabbit hops out from under a towering

fern and sits in front of Gwendolyn, twitching its nose and whiskers. Anna and Ivan watch silently as Gwendolyn turns to the animal.

"Hello! Nice to meet you, rabbit. My name is Gwendolyn," she says, putting her hand out to stroke the rabbit's ears. The rabbit does not move.

"And hello to you and to you!" she greets the chipmunks sitting beside her. "Do you all know each other? Rabbit, this is chipmunk and other chipmunk! Isn't the ground so lovely when the light dances on it? Wouldn't you say?"

"Are these your friends, Sibley?" Gwendolyn says, looking slightly up to her left, posing her question to someone who does not appear to be there.

She looks back towards her parents and giggles.

"Who is Sibley?" Ivan asks Anna. She shrugs and shakes her head, shushing him so he doesn't disturb the scene unfolding in front of them.

Gwendolyn is soon surrounded by a young fox, a badger, and a fawn.

She turns to each of the animals and greets them, nuzzling and patting her new friends.

The animals seem to be physically drawn from their hiding places right to Gwendolyn. *Is she that gentle?* wonders Anna. *That special?*

Not knowing what to do or say, Anna and Ivan wait a few minutes before approaching Gwendolyn. When they do, they startle the animals, making them scurry back to their hiding places in the forest.

Anna reaches for her daughter's small pink hand. "Come along now, Gwendolyn. We're almost there."

"Bye friends! Bye Sibley!" The child waves behind her.

"Who is Sibley, Gwendolyn?" asks Anna.

"My sister!" Gwendolyn replies, matter-of-factly, as she skips along ahead of her parents.

Speechless, Anna and Ivan stop walking. They had never told Gwendolyn about her sister.

Anna swallows and finds her voice. "Who told her,

Ivan? Who told her?"

VALORIUM IS a large, densely populated island in the Northern Sea. It would take a number of days to travel from one side of the island to the other. The western side of Valorium is a rocky mountain range, while the opposite side of the island is flat and mostly tree-covered.

The Caine family lives past the trees on the eastern end of the island, in a hut perched on a tall cliff by the sea. The Cellis live on the other side of the trees, about an hour's walk through the woods from the Caines.

The salty ocean air killed all of the grass on the Caine's thatched roof. To eight-year-old Lochlan, his home looks like it has blond hair like him.

Lochlan wishes he was out on the water with his father instead of being at home hanging laundry.

A thin column of smoke rises from his mother's cauldron into the clear blue sky. He hears the mournful cry of seagulls and the sound of waves crashing against the rocks below.

Lochlan pushes a piece of blond hair out of his face and shields his green eyes from the sun. He looks out at the ocean, trying to spot his father's fishing boat among the dozens that dot the sea. But all he sees are specks.

Sighing, he hangs another ratty old shirt on the clothesline.

"I had another one of those dreams last night, Mother," he says.

Rebecca Caine looks at him while stirring the concoction in her pot. "Another dream?" she says. Rebecca doesn't look like most witches. She does not have a beautiful face, but she is also not haggard. She is of an average build and height. Her thick red hair, the colour of rust, hangs to her waist, and a scarf tied around her head keeps the ocean breeze from tossing it into her pale green eyes.

Lochlan nods.

"Oh look!" she says, distracted. "You've perfected that one!"

"Yes, you might say I've got the hang of it!" says Lochlan, laughing. He points at a pair of his father's trousers in the basket at his feet. The pants stand up on their own, and, when Lochlan's index finger motions to the clothesline, they float up and cling to the line by their hems.

"Now, tell me about your dream while I stir the ashes in," says Rebecca.

Lochlan watches his mother add a scoop of ashes to the animal fat she is heating in her cauldron. He spots a fat toad sitting beside the cool dark entrance to the hut.

"I dreamt about a boy who looked just like me," he tells his mother.

Lochlan studies the toad, poking it gently with a soft blade of grass, careful not to get too close in case it was a goblin in disguise.

"In my dream, he was my brother and he was trying to tell me something. But when he spoke, I did not understand what he was saying."

Lochlan is too busy with the toad to see his mother's face twist in pain as she thinks of the child she lost eight years ago. She stops stirring and closes her eyes. The pain is as raw in this moment as it was on the morning she woke to find Lochlan's twin brother motionless beside her. This story is one she has never shared with her son.

Belly-down on the grass, Lochlan is face-to-face with the toad.

"Why do you think I would dream I had a brother?" Lochlan asks his mother.

Before Rebecca could think of how to answer her son, Lochlan loses interest in the conversation.

"I want to make this toad levitate," he says.

Rebecca composes herself. "You be careful, young man," she says, pushing away the grief. "I don't want you making any more animals disappear!"

"Will I ever be as powerful as you, Mother? As powerful as Elora?"

Lochlan had heard countless stories about his great ancestor Elora, a good witch who, once upon a time, vowed to keep the kingdom safe from dark magic by enchanting the village with a protection spell.

"I'm sure you can be at least as powerful as me, Lochlan," his mother tells him. "But there has not been a witch since Elora who could match her power. And I don't reckon there ever will be."

Lochlan sighs and extends his fingers in the direction of the toad.

Rebecca tosses a pinch of papery green leaves into her cauldron. The column of white smoke turns bright red, then white again. Rebecca wipes her hands on her apron as rectangular bars of soap leap from her pot and line themselves in a neat stack on the grass.

Lochlan closes his eyes and focuses all of his energy on the amphibian. He pictures it levitating. Lochlan opens his eyes and frowns. The toad is not floating. But it is wearing a dress.

Making a toad levitate would be so much better than hanging clothes, Lochlan thinks.

He looks behind him to see if his mother is watching him. She is not.

The leaves are changing colour on the trees that stand a stone's throw away from the Caines' hut. As Lochlan admires the orange and red leaves, he sees that the Celli family is walking through the opening to the woods.

"Why are they here?" Lochlan asks his mother.

Lochlan knows that the Cellis live on the other side of the forest, where you can't see the ocean. He would not want to live on that side of the island, where he couldn't imagine mermaids splashing in the waves.

"I have something to discuss with Mr. and Mrs. Celli, Lochlan. Go play with Gwendolyn while I speak with her parents."

Lochlan rolls his eyes. "Do I have to?"

"Take her to the shore, and see if you can find your father. If you spot him, tell him he needs to come and join us straight away."

"But she's a girl!"

"Be a good boy, and do as you're told," Rebecca says, steering her son towards the blue-eyed girl with rosy pink cheeks. She leans over and whispers in his ear, "Or I'll give you a tail."

Lochlan is sure his mother is joking, but as the son of a witch, he didn't want to take that chance.

CHAPTER THREE

Of Pure Heart and Magic Blood

"ANNA, IVAN! I'm so glad you've come," Rebecca greets her visitors. "Can I offer you both some tea?"

"Yes, please," says Anna, speaking for both herself and her husband.

Rebecca replaces the cauldron hanging over her fire with an iron kettle.

Gwendolyn shows Lochlan a field mouse in the palm of her hand.

"Has it become more noticeable?" Rebecca asks Anna, nodding to Gwendolyn. "Usually it does by this age."

"Why are the animals not afraid of her, Rebecca? Ivan and I watched her befriend a bevy of woodland creatures in the forest! Not one was timid of her!"

"Here, please, sit down." Rebecca motions to a mismatched set of twig chairs sitting near the entrance to the hut.

"What unusual furniture," Ivan says.

"Yes, the chairs are quite different, aren't they? Lochlan made them." She doesn't mention that he made the chairs by trying to make a tree disappear.

Lochlan has grown tired of the field mouse. He turns away from Gwendolyn and kicks a rock around the ground.

There are no homes around for miles. The Caines' hut sits high on a rocky cliff and is backed by the same old forest that surrounds the Cellis' home. The Caines' hut is the only one on this south-western corner of Valorium.

Rebecca calls to Lochlan, "Son, please take

Gwendolyn with you to look for your father. If it's ok with her parents?"

Anna and Ivan nod. Lochlan rolls his eyes and mopes towards the short path that leads from the hut to the shore. Gwendolyn skips along behind him.

"Rebecca, do you really believe that Lochlan and Gwendolyn should be married?" Anna asks once the children are out of sight.

"Not yet, of course, but yes. I do believe they must be betrothed," says Rebecca as she removes the kettle from its hook over the fire and fills three clay mugs with strong black tea.

"Ivan, Anna," Rebecca starts as she hands Anna and Ivan their tea, "young Gwendolyn is a pure heart."

"A what?" Anna has not heard of a *pure heart* before. Her husband shares her perplexed expression.

"Pure hearts are extremely rare," Rebecca explains, taking a drink of tea. Ivan and Anna hang on to her every word.

"I've been aware of the presence of a pure heart from

the moment Gwendolyn was born. I could sense the purity and goodness entering the world the moment she greeted you. I suspect it was an easy labour and that she didn't even cry."

Anna and Ivan nod their heads. Anna thinks back to the day her daughters were born. Gwendolyn had an angelic peace about her while her tiny sister cried and cried.

"I would also suspect she is an easy-going child?"

"Yes," Anna nods. "She never gives us any trouble."

Rebecca begins, "Pure hearts are born incapable of inflicting pain on others, including their mothers. They are not able to be cruel or hurtful. They are as good and kind as angels on Earth. They often glow as Gwendolyn does, giving off a special sort of light when they smile. You've already witnessed how her kindness attracts animals. I believe she can most likely hear them talk to her—at least those who have something to say, that is."

Anna's expression suggests concern. "Gwendolyn has brought nothing but joy since the moment we first laid our eyes on her," she says. "But, as a mother, I'm worried. Is this pure heart of hers going to put her in any danger?"

"I won't lie to you, Anna. It may. If the right wicked soul hears about Gwendolyn or sees her special light, they very well may wish to gain her heart. It holds a great deal of power. You must do your best to conceal it."

Anna gasps and throws her hands to her face, dropping her mug. It lands softly on the grass. Ivan puts his arm around his trembling wife. "Rebecca," he asks, "how are we to do that? How can we protect her?"

"That, Ivan, is one of the reasons I think she and Lochlan should marry. Lochlan is a kind boy, and he has magic blood, but he does not have dark magic in him. He will grow into a good man, I can assure you of that. I also believe he will be powerful enough to protect Gwendolyn later in life from any ill will that may come in her direction." Rebecca reaches down and picks the mug up off the ground, setting it in her lap.

"There is something else," Rebecca says.

Anna and Ivan watch Rebecca step into the hut, returning a moment later with a thick brown book.

"I'd hoped my Edmund would have been here before I spoke to you about this," she says. "But we could be waiting for him all day."

The book is plain, with a dark brown leather cover and a gold buckle on the front. *This must be her book of spells,* Anna thinks.

"Have you brought the sample?" Rebecca asks.

Anna nods and pulls a small glass jar from the pocket in the front of her dress.

"Wonderful," Rebecca exclaims. She takes the jar and holds it up to her face to study the dark red drop of Gwendolyn's blood. "You are surely both wondering why this was necessary."

"Yes," admits Ivan. "It was not a common request, to obtain a sample of our daughter's blood."

"There is an ancient prophecy that I believe is about to be fulfilled. I've brewed a potion that will confirm whether this is so. These are the final two ingredients." Rebecca reaches into her own pocket and pulls out a similar jar. She twists off the cover before placing it on her lap. "This is a drop of Lochlan's blood," she explains.

She pours Gwendolyn's blood into the vial with Lochlan's. She then pulls another glass jar from the pocket of her dress, this one containing a purple liquid. She carefully adds one drop of it to the blood. The mixture begins to glow.

Rebecca swirls the bottle, and Anna and Ivan watch as the concoction twinkles gold. Rebecca picks up her spell book and opens it to a blank page. She spills one drop of the potion onto the page before blowing on the parchment.

An image of the famous statue of Elora appears on the page.

Neither Anna nor Ivan have ever been to the Island of Rhyme where the statue stands. Nor have they ever seen a depiction of Elora. But they have heard stories about her since they were very young.

They stare at the image intensely, captivated by her beauty. Elora's hair falls to her waist in long soft waves, and her face wears an expression of angst. Her stone hands are outreached at her chest. A broken pendant hangs from her neck.

Words begin to appear, letter by letter, on the parchment.

Ivan and Anna hold hands as they read:

An intense darkness fell upon the kingdom of Falmoor many years ago, soon after the good witch Elora lost her twin sister, Calla.

According to the Legend of Rhyme, Elora, devastated by the loss of her twin, wept endlessly. Her spirit was so powerful and connected to the earth that the grief in her tears placed an accidental curse upon the kingdom. Her pain was so deep that all future twins were doomed to feel the same pain she had. Not a single set of twins has survived intact in the kingdom for at least a dozen generations. One of the babies always dies in infancy.

As the words continue to appear on the page, Anna speaks. "We know the legend, Rebecca. Of how Elora put a protection spell around the kingdom in the hopes it would prevent further evil from entering. And of how, as a young mother, Elora was betrayed and defeated by the dark wizard, Larque. He was not powerful enough to kill her. Instead, he'd conjured a spell that turned her to stone." She pauses. "Gwendolyn is a surviving twin."

Rebecca looks surprised. "Really? Gwendolyn had a twin? The other mustn't have been a pure heart or I would have sensed both when they were born." Rebecca pauses before saying, softly, "Lochlan also had a twin."

The three return their eyes to the words on the paper...

Lochlan Caine is of magic blood, the blood of the good and powerful Elora. Gwendolyn Celli is of the purest heart. Together they will produce a child more powerful than any human to have come before them. It is destined that Lochlan and Gwendolyn marry and produce this heir. For only the offspring of one with magic blood and a pure heart will be strong enough to lift the curse and to stop the babies from dying in their beds.

"Could there be some significance to Gwendolyn and Lochlan both being surviving twins? Won't this mean they're almost certain to give birth to twins of their own?" Anna asks.

Before Rebecca can give an answer, Lochlan and Gwendolyn come into view.

Anna looks at Lochlan. Could this boy become as great as his ancestor, Elora? Does he have what it will take to protect her daughter? Her future grandchildren?

Gwendolyn skips on the grass nearby, talking to herself.

"Mother," asks Lochlan, "is there cake?"

Anna smiles. For now, Lochlan is most definitely an ordinary eight-year-old boy.

"I believe so," says Rebecca. "But you must ask our guests if they would like something. Where are your manners?"

"No cake for us," Ivan says, rising from his seat. "The tea was lovely, Rebecca, but we really must be on our way so that we can discuss all of this."

"Yes," Anna agrees. "We will call again when we've reached our decision. Come along, Gwendolyn."

"Decision about what?" asks Lochlan, as the Cellis start to walk back to the woods behind the Caines' property.

"None of your concern, child," says Rebecca, brushing a strand of hair from her son's eyes. "At least not yet."

"Goodbye, Lochlan!" calls Gwendolyn, waving at her new friend.

Lochlan waves back and enters the hut, in search of cake.

That evening, after Gwendolyn falls asleep, Anna and Ivan sit by the fire and discuss the prophecy they were shown by Rebecca.

"He is a descendant of Elora," states Ivan. "If he can't keep our Gwendolyn safe, then we might as well lock her up. We must consent to this betrothal."

Anna nods in agreement. "As much as I would prefer Gwendolyn to grow up and choose the man she wishes to marry, learning about how vulnerable she is with a pure heart...well, we're left with no choice."

The couple goes to sleep that night, hoping they've made the right decision. Promising their only daughter to the son of a witch.

CHAPTER FOUR

A Secret Revealed

OVER THE years, Ivan and Anna did their best to hide Gwendolyn's pure heart from the world, though it was not easy. As she got older, Gwendolyn continued to grow more and more beautiful. The light that came from her was impossible to conceal. Regardless of how normal Ivan and Anna tried to pretend their daughter was, it was obvious there was something very special about her.

Luckily, no harm found Gwendolyn as a little girl. And before they knew it, Ivan and Anna Caine found themselves with a twelve-year-old daughter.

GWENDOLYN CAN'T quite reach the bottle of ointment her father asked her to fetch for him, so she stands on a chair to give her some extra height.

As she pulls the dusty brown bottle off the shelf, she notices a piece of paper tucked in the back, touching the wall. Wondering what it might be, she grabs for it before stepping back down from the chair to the ground.

She sets the ointment on the table and unfolds the paper she's found, expecting it to be a long-lost recipe or a letter from a relative.

We, Ivan and Anna Celli, herby agree to marry our daughter Gwendolyn Celli to Lochlan Caine, son of Edmund and Rebecca Caine, when both children reach the age of majority.

Gwendolyn suddenly feels faint. *Am I really reading a marriage contract?* she thinks. *And who is Lochlan Caine?*

She now starts to experience an emotion she hasn't felt before. It can only be anger.

REBECCA CAINE hurries to the corner of her hut. Near the counter on which she prepares the family's meals hangs an old wooden cabinet. Its shelves hold all of her precious jars of herbs and spices for cooking.

Sensing that Gwendolyn Celli is nearby, there's something Rebecca must prepare this morning, but it's not breakfast.

She must work quickly. Her fourteen-year-old son, Lochlan, is outside feeding the chickens and collecting their eggs. He will be back within minutes.

Standing in front of the cabinet, she flicks her fingers in its direction. It promptly detaches itself from the wall and slowly turns itself around, revealing three shelves of small glass bottles. Rebecca's hands, still extended in the direction of the cabinet, make a pushing motion, prompting it to again attach itself to the wall.

One of the bottles is empty. She picks it up and sets it on the counter next to her book of spells, which is opened to a potion recipe. Carefully checking the list of ingredients, she turns to the cabinet and selects three bottles. Two of them contain liquids—one is glowing purple and the other is clear—while the third contains what looks like strands from golden spider webs.

Rebecca picks up the empty glass bottle and carefully

pours three drops of purple liquid inside. She then adds one drop of clear liquid. The potion fizzes and bubbles. Using a long, thin wooden stick, she takes a strand of the golden threads in the third bottle and adds it to the concoction. She then taps the glass and swirls its contents around. A pink mist curls up and out of the bottle. The potion is finished.

FATHER CAN get his own ointment, Gwendolyn thinks. *I need to get some air.*

Red-faced and light-headed, she scoops up her bag and slings it over her shoulder. She storms out of the hut towards the forest. To the place where she does her best thinking.

After ambling along the logging trail for close to an hour, Gwendolyn reaches her favourite spot. Off the side of the path is a circle of tall oak trees. The lush forest floor here is littered with acorns, and the air is filled with the chatter of squirrels.

She plods along over felled trees and moss-covered logs to reach the hugging trees—at least that's what she's always called them.

Two of the ten oak trees that grow in a circle here appear to have grown holding each other. Their branches reach out and wrap around together. Gwendolyn gathers the skirts of her dress in one hand and carefully climbs up to the place where the branches meet, sitting in the middle of the trees' hug.

It is almost completely quiet. Gwendolyn feels at home here. She reaches into her cloth bag and pulls out a book of parchment and a writing quill. She jumps at the sound of a woodpecker pounding its beak into one of the trees she sits in as she turns to an empty page in her diary.

REBECCA ADMIRES the pink liquid she has concocted. It smells sweet, like boiling sugar.

She reaches now for the quiver of arrows leaning against the wall. She pulls out all six arrows and dips each of them into the potion before placing them back in their holder.

After returning all of the glass   bottles to the shelf, Rebecca once again flicks her fingers at the cabinet. It detaches itself from the wall and turns around again, revealing Rebecca's everyday cooking ingredients.

Rebecca wipes her hands on her apron and closes her spell book, satisfied that she's managed to charm the arrows before Lochlan finishes his chores.

She had no choice but to tamper with fate.

STEADYING HERSELF in the tree, Gwendolyn twists the lid off her small bottle of ink. After carefully dipping her quill in the bottle, she starts to write. But before she puts down a word, she hears a twig snap somewhere nearby. Gwendolyn looks up from her page. She usually has the forest to herself. *Probably a deer*, she thinks.

LOCHLAN PULLS an arrow from the quiver on his back and places it in the bow. The unsuspecting partridge is about twelve paces away, in clear view. Steadying the bow in his left hand, Lochlan pulls the arrow back with his right. Focusing in on his target, he releases the arrow, which slices the air and heads straight for the bird.

But before the arrow hits its target, it stops in mid air and veers off to the right into the woods. Lochlan scratches his head in disbelief at what he has witnessed.

"You are one lucky partridge," Lochlan tells the bird that's now racing for cover under the trees. "I never miss that badly."

Slinging the quiver of arrows back over his shoulder, he mutters to himself, "I don't understand. Where did that arrow fly off to?"

AS GWENDOLYN puts her quill to paper again, she is interrupted by the whoosh of an arrow punching through the air. She looks up and sees a flash of blue as that arrow abruptly changes direction, narrowly missing her head, and lands in the branch she's leaning on.

She turns to the left and sees that the head of the arrow has pierced the tree, inches from her face.

Her heart pounds. Not wanting to spend another minute in this tree, she twists the cover onto her bottle of ink and carefully closes her diary before slipping it into her bag. She jumps out of the tree, so shocked that she doesn't notice the fine pink mist curling up and around the arrow like smoke.

CHAPTER FIVE

An Enchanted Encounter

THAT PARTRIDGE would have made a delicious supper, Lochlan thinks as he walks further down the path. He walks to the place where the partridge stood just seconds ago. There's a clearing off to the right, where his arrow had flown.

Lochlan had walked this path more times than he could count during his life, and he never before noticed this spot.

He doesn't see where his arrow has landed, though, because he's noticed he's not alone here in the forest.

Lochlan sees a girl, one who looks to be his age, jump

down out of a tree. She picks up a bag off the ground and hangs it over her shoulder. She starts to walk in Lochlan's direction and soon notices him. She jumps back, startled to see him.

"Hello?" she says.

"Hello," Lochlan echoes the girl's greeting.

Noticing the bow in his hands, the girl gestures up to the tree and says, "Were you looking for this?"

Lochlan sees his arrow is stuck in the tree that the girl has jumped out of. "Yes!" he says. "I'm glad it didn't hit you!"

"Me too!" the girl agrees. "Being stabbed by an arrow would have ruined my day. By the way, my name is Gwendolyn."

"I'm Lochlan," he replies.

Neither of the two recall meeting each other six years ago.

"What exactly were you aiming at?" Gwendolyn asks.

"There was a partridge on the path, but my arrow took off in this direction. It was very strange," Lochlan explains.

"Well, it didn't hit me, so no harm done!" Gwendolyn smiles as she starts to walk past Lochlan.

He isn't sure why, but Lochlan doesn't want to stop talking to this girl. He likes looking at her, with her long brown hair and bright blue eyes. And she has a pretty smile. *How can I try and make her stay here to talk with me some more?* he thinks.

"I have a lunch with me. Are you hungry?" he asks.

Gwendolyn stops walking. "I just finished a snack."

"Oh, ok," Lochlan says.

Am I imagining things, or did he sound disappointed? "But, it is quite some time until supper. Maybe I could have a small bite," Gwendolyn smiles.

A shy grin tugs at the corners of Lochlan's lips. He reaches into the pocket on his trousers and pulls out a slab of something wrapped in brown paper.

"Shall we sit down?" Gwendolyn suggests.

"Sure," Lochlan says. He sets down his bow and arrows before sitting down on the squishy forest floor beside Gwendolyn. She places her bag on the ground in front of her.

As Lochlan unwraps the brown paper covering his snack, Gwendolyn notices his hands are shaking. She notices because hers are, too. She wonders if his heart is beating fast like hers. And if he also has butterflies in his stomach.

"What's in the bag?" Lochlan asks as he offers the honey cake to Gwendolyn.

Gwendolyn breaks off a piece of cake. Before biting into it, she tells him, "It's just my diary. I like to come here and think and write sometimes."

But Lochlan doesn't hear her. He is distracted by the many small animals that have come out from their hiding places in the forest. Surrounding Gwendolyn is a fawn, a raccoon, a rabbit, and several squirrels. He decides that perhaps he isn't the only one quite taken by Gwendolyn's beauty and the kindness that seems to radiate from her.

"Are you thirsty?" Gwendolyn asks. "I have some water in my canteen."

She reaches into her bag and her face crumples. "No!" she cries, pulling out her diary, which is soaked with water. "My canteen mustn't have been closed. My diary," she stammers, "it's ruined."

"Here," Lochlan reaches for the book, "I think I can help."

"How can you help? It's ruined." Gwendolyn opens the book to reveal that the ink on most of the pages is no longer legible.

Lochlan knows he's not supposed to use magic in front of ordinary people, but he does not believe that Gwendolyn is ordinary. And seeing her cry is causing an ache in his heart. He has to help.

He takes the diary from Gwendolyn's hands and opens it on his lap. He holds his hands, palm down, over the wet pages.

Closing his eyes, Lochlan does as his mother has taught him, and concentrates on the strong feelings he has at this moment about Gwendolyn and helping to fix her book.

"Sicco!" The word rolls out of Lochlan's mouth. The pages of the diary on his lap rustle as a heat radiates from Lochlan's hands. Gwendolyn watches in awe as her words appear back on their pages.

The diary appears to be exactly as it was before it was soaked by her canteen.

When Lochlan opens his eyes, he looks down at the diary and is surprised to see that his magic worked. He smiles widely and hands the book to Gwendolyn. She instinctively throws her arms around her new friend. "Thank you so much!" she exclaims.

Lochlan smiles, and his face turns a bright shade of pink.

Back at the Caine's hut, Rebecca gazes into the pink potion she brewed earlier. She smiles as she looks at the scene of her son and Gwendolyn Celli sitting on the forest floor. The spell has worked.

FROM THAT day on, Gwendolyn and Lochlan did not leave each other's thoughts. They lived at opposite sides of that old logging trail, with Lochlan living near the sea, and Gwendolyn in a hut nestled by trees, with a view of the mountains. But they would meet in that same spot by the hugging trees as often as they could until they grew into young adults.

Neither of them ever dared to remove the arrow from the tree. It reminded them of their obvious destiny to meet.

Then one day, in that very place, with the sun shining through the hugging trees, Lochlan asked Gwendolyn to be his wife.

Soon after they were wed, there was a baby on the way.

CHAPTER SIX

Visit from Elora

LOCHLAN IS almost asleep when he hears his wife whisper to him in the dark, "Lochlan?"

"Yes?"

"What if I'm carrying twins?"

Lochlan reaches for Gwendolyn's hand. "We shall worry about that when the time comes. For now, try to get some rest."

That night, Elora appears to Lochlan in a dream.

She floats above the ground against a backdrop of

black, her golden hair hanging around her shoulders. Her creamy white skin glows, and long white skirts flow behind her.

"Lochlan," she warns, "The Legend is not true. There is a man to be blamed for the dead children. You are of my blood. If Gwendolyn is to give birth to twins, there is but one place you and your family will be safe and that is near me at my final resting place on the Island of Rhyme.

"Before I was entrapped in my grave of stone, I banished Larque so he could never enter Rhyme. It is he who is to blame. It is he who should be feared. Please, bring your wife here near me. It will give me comfort as I anguish in limbo, and you and your family will have protection from him. You must heed my words."

Lochlan wakes, trying to make sense of what just happened. He has never had a visitation from Elora before. Sleep doesn't find him again this night.

The next morning, when Lochlan tells Gwendolyn about Elora's message, she doesn't even pause. Touching her belly, she states, "We must leave today."

Lochlan helps Gwendolyn pack their few belongings.

They say goodbye to their parents and make the day-long journey to the small island on the edge of the kingdom.

Gwendolyn and Lochlan are hopeful that the darkness will not find them here.

They are mistaken.

CHAPTER SEVEN

Island of Secrets

THE COUPLE settles in an idyllic spot on the southern side of the island, near the sea. From their new property, they have a beautiful view of the sea to the east, a rocky mountain range to the west, and there is an old hardwood forest nearby as well that provides shelter from the wind.

"Are you sure you don't need my help?" Gwendolyn asks Lochlan as he assembles the reeds and other supplies needed to build the roof for their hut.

"I'm sure," he assures her. From within the stone structure he has constructed over the past couple of days, Lochlan uses his magic to frame the roof. He points to the reeds like a conductor, and they float up above him, putting themselves in place and providing a support for the grass sods he will add later. "I've got this covered," he says with a smile.

When Lochlan was gathering the stones for the walls of their home, he had placed an enchantment in them so that evil could not enter, in case Elora's strength alone was not enough to protect their family.

Gwendolyn prays it will be one of Lochlan's successful spells and not one that "isn't quite right."

"I think I'll go for a walk," she says. "I believe there's a mill over in the village. I will bring some wheat with me. Perhaps we can have bread tomorrow."

"Oh," says Lochlan. "I brought in some of the wheat earlier. He steps away from his roofing materials and goes to the sheath of wheat that leans against a wall. "Let me save you the trip. Baking bread is an easy trick!"

While holding the wheat, Lochlan closes his eyes and recites a spell, the words of which Gwendolyn can't quite understand.

The wheat is transformed, but not in the way Lochlan

has intended.

"I don't think those will go well with eggs," Gwendolyn teases.

Lochlan frowns at the pink roses in his arms. "Perhaps you should see if you can find some flour in the village."

Gwendolyn walks along, carrying the wheat in a sack that hangs from her shoulder. She can't help but wonder why her husband can build a home, but he can not bake bread. Why he can manipulate objects, but not transform them. She tells herself she'll bring it up with Rebecca one day.

The sky feels huge on this small island, and she feels at ease here. There are no other dwellings on the edge of Rhyme where she and Lochlan have settled. The islanders all live on the other side of the stream, closer to the merchants. She and Lochlan chose to live where there would be more privacy—in the hopes that evil would have a harder time finding them.

She walks to the giant old tree that stands a short distance from where Lochlan has built their hut.

She is drawn to the tree, though she can't explain

why. She stops to admire it for awhile before continuing. She enjoys the sound of the stream.

The stream runs through the entire island. It starts as a waterfall in the mountain range at the western side of the island and winds like a blue ribbon all the way to the east where it empties into the sea. The tree is on the same side of the stream as Lochlan and Gwendolyn's home.

Gwendolyn continues toward the mill, crossing the stream on a small wooden footbridge.

When she is on the other side of the stream, she walks past the statue of Elora. Unlike the tree, she is not drawn to it. In fact, she feels very much like not approaching it at all.

She doesn't have to walk very far past the bridge to reach the mill. But, before she enters with her wheat, she is distracted by a mouth-watering aroma.

What is that wonderful smell? she wonders.

Gwendolyn suddenly feels ravenous. She walks in the direction of the smell, finding herself at a small wooden dwelling only a few steps away. It is a home between the blacksmith and the mill, and there is something sitting in the window that Gwendolyn does not recognize.

She approaches the hut and takes in the delicious sweet scent.

"Are you hungry, my dear?" A woman with a kind face speaks to her while sweeping the entrance of her hut.

"Oh! I am so sorry!' Gwendolyn apologizes. "But I have never smelled anything like this before. What do you call it?"

The food is round with a golden brown surface. Small holes have been sliced into it, revealing something red beneath. Steam rises from the holes in the topping.

The woman laughs. "It is called a pie, and it tastes even better than it smells! Would you like to try a slice, my dear?"

"Oh, I would hate to impose," Gwendolyn says, though she wants nothing more at this moment than to taste the pie.

"I insist. I happen to have another pie inside that's

already cooled. And I just made a pot of tea. My name is Novah," the woman says, extending a hand to Gwendolyn.

"Gwendolyn," she says, shaking Novah's hand. "And I'd love to have tea with you. Thank you."

Gwendolyn follows Novah inside.

Novah's face is unwrinkled, but her hair is coarse and grey. She is much shorter than Gwendolyn, but she appears to have the agility of a child. Her warm, brown eyes seem to hold many years of wisdom. She does not walk like an old person walks.

Gwendolyn and the woman chat like old friends while they sip their tea and eat the wild cherry pie—the most delicious thing Gwendolyn has ever tasted.

When Novah asks Gwendolyn what has brought her to Rhyme, Gwendolyn answers with a note of concern in her voice, "We moved here because my husband believes it will be a good, safe place to live."

"When do you expect your baby?" Novah asks.

"Oh," exclaims Gwendolyn, "I didn't think it had

become obvious yet!" She places her hands over her stomach, which had not yet swelled from the pregnancy.

Novah laughs. "Oh, child, when you get to be my age, you develop a sense for some things."

Gwendolyn wanted so badly to ask Novah how old she was, but she would never ask such an impolite question to a woman who was clearly her elder.

"I'm not entirely sure when the baby will come, but I expect I'm a few months along."

"You've made a wise decision to settle here, Gwendolyn. Rhyme is a wonderful place to live," remarks Novah, bringing the last few crumbs of pie to her mouth. "There is something in the air that keeps us young."

"What do you mean?" Gwendolyn asks between bites of sweet, gooey, flakey pie.

"Well," Novah starts, her eyes twinkling when she speaks, "I have been healthy every day of my life, and I'll be two hundred years old this month."

Gwendolyn drops her fork. "I'm sorry," she says. "Did

you say… you're two hundred years old?"

"Almost," Novah nods and takes a sip of tea.

"But you look like you're my mother's age, like a woman of forty!"

"We all live very long, wonderful lives here!" Novah declares.

"How in the world is that possible?" Gwendolyn asks.

"Like I said, dear. There's just something in the air here in Rhyme. Can't you feel it? My mother was much older than me when she passed. I think you were wise to bring your family here."

"I hope you're right!" says Gwendolyn.

"But there is a legend," Novah proceeds, "that when people leave the island, their health deteriorates and they start to show their age."

She pauses. "If I were to leave Rhyme now, I would most likely drop dead suddenly of old age. Now, how about that!"

"Has anyone tested this legend?" questions Gwendolyn.

"Not in my lifetime," Novah replies. "And I'm not about to test it now."

Gwendolyn notices by the light outside that the sun has started to set. "Oh dear, I should be going, Novah. But I do hate to leave!"

"Yes, dear, you better be on your way. Lochlan is sure to worry," she says.

"I hope I will see you again," Gwendolyn smiles. "I'm sure you have many stories to tell."

"Indeed I do, dear. Please come and visit anytime. There is always tea and pie."

It is too late for Gwendolyn to visit the mill.

She thinks about Novah as she walks home. *Did I tell her Lochlan's name?* she wonders. She shrugs this detail off, deciding she must have. *What an endearing old soul,* she thinks.

Gwendolyn passes the metalsmith's shop and the

church before reaching the footbridge that will lead her back home. When she reaches the other side of the stream, she stumbles over a rock.

Before she falls, she sees a flash of blue light and feels something catch her. She manages to correct herself without being hurt. She looks around to see if anyone had been around to see the blue light. But she was alone.

Pregnancy is doing strange things to me, she thinks. *Now I'm becoming clumsy and am seeing things.*

WHEN GWENDOLYN arrives home, there is a new roof on the hut. Lochlan is sitting inside on the dirt floor with some scraps of wood, a length of wool, and a few bits of iron.

"I have to tell you about this amazing woman I met, Loch." Gwendolyn notices the array of materials sitting in front of her husband. "What are you doing?"

"Oh," Lochlan says, "I was going to make us a table and chairs. Go on and tell me about this woman."

He flips the pages of his well-worn grimoire—his book

of spells—and sets it down beside him. He holds his hand over the scraps and starts to speak, "Mensa Lignum."

"She was amazing," Gwendolyn starts, as she sets the sheath of wheat on the floor next to Lochlan. "She's almost two hundred years old! She told me Rhyme has some sort of magic in the air. That people don't get sick and they live extraordinarily long lives!"

"I've never heard such a thing," says Lochlan. "Do you believe her? Or do you think she has lost her marbles?"

"Oh I believe her. I have a sense about her," Gwendolyn declares.

But Lochlan doesn't hear his wife's words for he is deep in thought, concentrating on his spell.

Within moments, the wood, wool, and iron are gone and a fat white chicken stands in their place.

CHAPTER EIGHT

A Bird in the Hand

LOCHLAN'S AXE comes down upon a large stick, splitting it clean in two with a large crack. He wipes the sweat from his forehead with the back of his hand, picks up another stick from the large woodpile, and sets it on the tree stump he uses as a chopping block.

"It's too hot for this," he mumbles to himself, bringing the axe down to rest. "Aqua," he commands. A cup floats from the ground up to his hand. He brings it to his lips and drinks. He spits out a mouthful of warm water before putting his finger in the cup. "Frigidus!" he says while stirring the water.

He feels the water turn from warm to cold, and he

once again brings the cup to his lips. "That's better," he remarks, after taking a long, refreshing drink.

Lochlan studies his surroundings. A volcano stands tall in the distance, just past the mountains that stand on the western side of the island. The lava fields, formed from eruptions of the long dormant volcano, make such a bumpy landscape, it looks as though someone has placed a thick green blanket of grass over a field of uneven boulders. There are no other dwellings on this side of the island, but across the stream and off in the distance, the rolling green hills are spotted with dull grey huts.

On this particular morning in late August, all of the islanders have gathered near the old tree, not far from Lochlan and Gwendolyn's hut. But the people are watching the tree, not Lochlan.

I can make this job easier, Lochlan thinks to himself. He pauses to remember the correct spell.

Gwendolyn, who has been picking wild berries, takes a break to watch her husband work.

"Did you say it's too hot for that?" she asks, selecting a deep purple berry from the basket next to her and popping it in her mouth. "You've only chopped three sticks!"

Lochlan looks at the pile of wood waiting to be chopped and then points at the axe. "I guess I'm not used to back-breaking labour." The axe proceeds to chop the wood, completely on its own accord, as sticks float to the chopping block, one by one.

Satisfied, Lochlan sits down next to his wife on the grass. He takes a handful of berries from the basket and shoves them in his mouth. "Mmmm, you're sure these aren't poisonous?" he asks, chewing the sweet juicy flesh of the perfectly ripe berries.

"We'll find out in a minute," Gwendolyn smiles, tucking a long strand of dark brown hair behind her ear.

She gestures toward the crowd gathered near the tree. "The people are starting to arrive for the butterflies! Wouldn't it be lovely if the baby came today?"

She places Lochlan's hands on her belly. "There is not as much kicking. I think she's running out of room."

Lochlan's hands are met with little thumps of baby elbows, feet, or knees (who could really say for sure which parts were shoving around in there?), and he is so intent on the brute strength of his baby son or daughter that he doesn't notice the watchful eyes of a fat toad from beside the woodpile.

"Your mother keeps telling me you're a little girl and that is just fine by me, as long as there is only one of you," Lochlan speaks to Gwendolyn's belly.

"Oh, Loch, did you hear that?"

"Did I hear what?" asks Lochlan, listening for a sound.

Then the noise reaches his ears. A tiny chirping from behind the berry bushes next to their hut.

Gwendolyn lifts herself off the soft grass. Her pale creamy skin is flushed from the heat. It is getting harder and harder to carry her growing belly around.

Gwendolyn carefully makes her way around the shrubs where the wild berries grow, and there on the mossy ground is a small sparrow. The bird lifts one wing while trying to flap the other.

"Oh! You poor little thing," she whispers as she gently picks up the bird. "Here, let's have a look at you."

"Oh, I wish I could do something to help you, you sweet thing," she says, frowning at the small creature trembling in her hand. Gwendolyn sets the bird on her belly with her hands wrapped around its body. "Loch, is there anything you can do?"

"No, Gwen, you know I can't heal." Lochlan looks down at the bird.

Unable to bear the sadness of his wife, Lochlan puts his hand on the bird as Gwendolyn gently strokes its lame wing. He closes his eyes.

The sparrow starts to vibrate and grow warm. A beam of light radiates from the bird's wing. Gwendolyn remains silent, afraid to break the spell.

Lochlan opens his eyes. The bird shakes as if it has a chill in its tiny body, before flapping both wings. He gives a slight nod as if to thank his rescuers, and, just like that, the bird flies off to the tree to join the crowd of people waiting for the glass wing butterflies to arrive as they do every year on this day.

Lochlan smiles.

"What was that?" questions Gwendolyn. *Did we cause something to happen to that bird, Lochlan and I?* Gwendolyn wonders if her unborn child has played a role in whatever magic was taking place before her eyes.

"I'm not entirely sure, but I wonder... Could your pure heart and my magic blood have created a healing force?" asks Lochlan.

"Perhaps. If that's the case, what sort of powerful person do we have growing in there?" Gwendolyn asks, looking at her belly.

A fat toad watches Gwendolyn and Lochlan with great interest. His thin black lips curve into a smile, and he hops, unnoticed, back to the old tree where the onlookers stand.

CHAPTER NINE

A Gilded Girl

WHEN SIBLEY leaves the pixie tree that morning, she flies through a cloudless sky, greeting songbirds along the way. She enjoys listening to them sing as she travels the short distance to Gwendolyn's hut.

She takes a deep breath of salty air before coming in for a gentle landing on the ledge of one of the hut's two windows.

Inside, Sibley can see that Lochlan and Gwendolyn are busy getting to know their new family members.

The thin straw mattress they sleep on is piled with felted wool blankets and animal skins. It looks soft and comfortable for Gwendolyn and the babies. Sibley smiles.

She looks forward to watching the baby girl grow up. She is her watcher, as she was Gwendolyn's.

The baby boy has a watcher fairy as well, but Sibley doesn't see him anywhere.

Sibley watches Gwendolyn study her silent little girl with a concerned expression on her face. The baby looks at her mother with bright, wide eyes. "Lochlan," Gwendolyn turns to her husband, "shouldn't she have cried by now?"

"Oh, she hasn't had any reason to be upset yet. Besides," he says, looking down at the red-faced baby in his own arms, "this little fella has been doing enough crying for both of them!"

Sibley smiles as Lochlan kisses Gwendolyn's forehead.

"They're both so perfect," Gwendolyn beams, "I can't bear to think about losing one of them."

"Nothing is going to happen to them, Gwendolyn," Lochlan reassures his wife.

"I have never wanted so badly for you to be right. Here," Gwendolyn gently lifts the warm little baby girl she is holding and hands her to Lochlan, "you hold them both for a minute. I will make us some tea."

Finally, Sibley thinks, preparing to make her move. *They'll have to take their eyes off the babies for a minute!*

"Let me do that," urges Lochlan. He lowers the babies to the bedding on the floor and nods in the direction of the hearth, and the coals glow red. He waves his hand at the iron kettle and it lowers itself over the coals.

Oh, for Heaven's sake, Sibley says to herself. *Magic to make a cup of tea? Well, it's now or never!*

Sibley zooms into the hut and makes a beeline for the baby girl.

Gwendolyn smiles. "Honestly, Loch, you know I'm quite capable of boiling the kettle."

"Nonsense, you need your rest."

When the kettle starts boiling, Lochlan nods to two clay mugs. The kettle removes itself from the fire and pours two cups of tea.

"Sweet baby girl," Sibley whispers in the baby's ear. "There is so much weight on your tiny shoulders, but I will always be here for you." Sibley blows into her hands and then places them on the infant's head above her left ear, marking the child.

Gwendolyn catches a glimmer of blue light out of the corner of her eye. That same little blink of light she has seen from time to time, for as long as she can remember.

"Lochlan, did you see that?"

"Did I see what?"

The blue light is long gone. "Oh, nothing," Gwendolyn says.

Back on the ledge of the window, Sibley sees that the boy is still crying.

Lochlan scoops up the babies and sits beside his wife. "Little ones," he coos, "what shall we name you?"

He runs his fingers through his little girl's thick head of black hair. "Gwendolyn!" he exclaims. "Would you look at this!"

With an anxious expression on her face, Gwendolyn leans in to see what her husband has found.

There, within the shock of black hair on the baby's head, is a small patch of silver. Gwendolyn carefully strokes the hair and turns to her husband.

"Our daughter is marked for greatness, Lochlan!"

Sibley smiles.

"We will call her Ariana," Lochlan states, "our precious silver girl."

"And you," says Gwendolyn to the baby boy who is still crying, "you will be Asher. A name that means happy, so that perhaps you will live your life in a better mood than you were in when you entered the world!"

With Asher crying and Ariana bright-eyed and smiling, Lochlan sets them both down on the straw mat to get a better look at them.

"Let us pray that they will be safe," voices Gwendolyn with a tear rolling down her cheek into her tea cup.

Sibley wishes she could go in and reassure Gwendolyn that everything would be ok, like she had when she was a little girl. But it was no use. Gwendolyn had outgrown her belief in fairies, and hadn't seen or heard Sibley in many years.

"What did I miss?" A fairy with rusty red hair and a spattering of freckles lands beside Sibley.

"Cinnamon, hello!" Sibley says. "They have named the babies. Mine is Ariana and yours is Asher. Take care of him."

Cinnamon nods. "I'll take it from here," he says.

Before Sibley heads back to the pixie tree to tell Calla of Coraira that she's completed her assignment, she watches with astonishment as Ariana reaches for her brother's hand.

When the pair of tiny hands grasp each other, Asher instantly stops crying and Ariana's new streak of silver hair softly glows.

CHAPTER TEN

A Plan is Hatched

LARQUE PULLS a black hood over his thick grey hair before exiting the damp, dark cave carved out of the mountainside on the island of Valorium. The hood hides his grotesquely scarred face.

Each time Larque tries to leave the rocky terrain of the mountains, his skin singes and burns. Marks of Elora's curse.

He'd stopped bothering long ago, leaving his work to Grimblerod. This time, though, the goblin would not be able to help separate Rhyme's latest set of twins. Lochlan Caine has placed an enchantment on his hut, preventing Larque or Grimblerod or any evil force from snatching one of his babies.

Larque needs that child more than any of the souls he's collected over the years. Born of a pure heart and a magician, there is no telling the power in the marked one.

Sitting on a felled log beside his fire pit, Larque gestures to the cold ashes in front of him, conjuring up a great flame.

Earlier that day, one of his snares trapped a rabbit. Larque has already cleaned and skinned the animal, and he now places it on a metal spit to roast over the fire.

While the flame dances beneath his dinner, he looks up to the smoke curling into the sky.

An image comes into view of the Caine babies in the secluded hut on the southeastern corner of Rhyme. But two more images appear, other households in the kingdom, both here on the large island of Valorium, where twins have been born.

Larque reaches into the leather pouch that hangs from his belt. His fingers move around more than a hundred smooth pebbles, one for each child he's taken. It pleases and comforts him to feel the stones in his hand and think of those stolen lives. Each time a twin enters the world, he rolls the smooth pebbles around in his hands and finds peace with what he must do.

He looks up at the sky. It is a crescent moon tonight. He must wait before sending Grimblerod the signal.

He smells the meat roasting on the fire and realizes how hungry he is. He turns the rabbit so it cooks on its other side.

"If I can't get to the child," he mutters, "I must make the child come to me." The sound of his voice surprises him. He can't remember the last time he heard himself speak.

CHAPTER ELEVEN

Inside the Pixie Tree

FIDGET SITS in her favourite mossy nook and tries to turn off her mind long enough for a nap. But when her pointy elfin ears hear what sounds like a million tiny fingers snapping, she races for the window in the pixie tree.

"It's time! It's time!" she squeaks excitedly in her tiny pixie voice as she looks out upon thousands of glass wing butterflies flapping their translucent wings. The pixie tree is a stop on the butterflies' yearly migration, a favourite event for all of the islanders, even the pixies.

"Anyone?" she says, looking to her left and to her right for someone with whom she can watch the spectacle.

When nobody answers, Fidget shrugs her shoulders and bounces back to the opening in the pixie tree to watch the butterflies land within its branches.

Standing approximately four inches tall, Fidget is dressed in a skirt made from a tiger lily bloom and a shirt fashioned out of the remnants of an abandoned cocoon. Her white hair is braided on each side of her tiny head.

Thousands of magnificently coloured butterflies circle the tree, making it look like the tree is wearing a costume.

"Move!" Fidget says, waving to the butterflies obstructing her view from the window. "I can't see you with you in the way!"

Frustrated, Fidget wiggles her ears and pinches her nose to change the view from the watching place.

"What are you looking at?" another woodland pixie whispers in Fidget's ear, intentionally scaring her.

"AAAAAAAAAHHHHH!!!!!!" Fidget spins herself around, coming face-to-face with Wink, with his bright red cheeks and sneaky, beady eyes.

"What is wrong with you?" screams Fidget, smacking Wink on the back of the head, further messing up his scruffy brown hair.

Wink is too busy laughing to answer Fidget, and his laughter causes Fidget to burst into giggles as well.

"Hey!" shouts Wink, pointing to a fat toad hopping over to the tree. "Is that who I think it is?"

Fidget and Wink watch Grimblerod, in toad form, hop around the human world. The goblin was heading for Gwendolyn and Lochlan's thatched stone hut about one hundred paces (or ten thousand hops) away.

"What is he doing out when there are so many feet around?" squeals Fidget, motioning towards the crowd of villagers surrounding the tree.

"Who knows what he's up to," muses Wink. "But whatever it is, it's probably nothing good."

"That's awfully brave of him, isn't it?" quips Fidget. "Why is he always snooping around their place? What's he so interested in?"

She pauses and says, "With nobody at home, he should be poking around those huts, finding out where the villagers are keeping the good stuff. But, look! He's heading back below."

Wink tilts his head and puts a finger to his cheek. "Fidget! Are you thinking what I'm thinking?"

"That you smell like rotten troll breath?" says Fidget, covering her nose with the slim fingers on her little hand.

"Try again, Fidget," says Wink, shaking his head.

Fidget takes a deep breath and sniffs. "Nope. Still troll."

Wink sighs loudly. "Fidget, if all the villagers are here at the tree, we could go and play as many tricks as we like! We might even be able to find some biscuits for supper." He brings a hand to his belly and licks his lips.

"What are we waiting for?" exclaims Fidget.

The pair pinch their noses, wiggle their ears, and exit the tree in a flash of blue light.

"Aaacchoo!"

"Oh!" says Fidget, shaking her head and wriggling her nose. She looks back towards the tree and turns to Wink. "That always makes me sneeze!"

Neither Fidget nor Wink have wings, but they can bounce very high. They zip and bounce along the ground, dodging hundreds of feet on their way to where the humans live.

"You're lucky Coraira's magic protects us from being seen, Fidget!" voices Wink as his friend makes faces at all of the humans she sees.

"Sibley!" says Wink, gesturing to two young fairies peering in the wood-shuttered window of the Caines' hut.

Fidget squints at the hut coming closer into view. *I wonder what she's doing there.*

"Sibley! Why aren't you watching the butterflies?" Fidget leaps up to the ledge where Sibley sits and peeks in the window.

"What are you two doing here?" Sibley asks. "I hope

you're not causing any mischief!"

Woodland pixies find great delight in causing mischief. Fairies do not.

"Of course not, of course not," lies Wink, nodding his head. "But we should be moving on, shouldn't we, Fidget? Sibley... you should keep watching what you're watching, and you should probably not worry about what we're doing."

"Is that your girl, Sibley?" Fidget asks her blue-haired friend.

"Yes," says Sibley. "Gwendolyn has grown up into such a lovely human. And now she's a mother, I can hardly believe it."

"What does she smell like?" asks Fidget. "Wink says humans smell like ogre bottoms. Is that true?"

Fidget runs off after Wink out of sight of their fairy friend.

Because there are no other huts around, Wink and Fidget race off across the stream. They leap over the uneven grass to the huts where no one is home. Moving quite nimbly, Wink quickly switches undergarments from clothesline to clothesline.

After all of the laundry has been swapped between neighbours, he steps back and admires his work, smiling and laughing.

Fidget stands beside a neat vegetable patch ready to be harvested. She yanks orange carrots, yellow onions, and purple beets up from the ground. "Upsie daisy!" she says, planting the vegetables upside down in neat rows.

CHAPTER TWELVE

Asher Hunts a Dragon

I AM four years old and so is my sister. We are picking vegetables with Mother and Father, but I don't like picking vegetables if you want to know the truth.

Father says one day he will show me how he picks vegetables with his magic so they pick themselves, but now he needs to teach me and Ariana hard work.

I would rather learn magic.

I swing my sword that is actually a stick. I say, "I'm the brave knight Asher and I slaved the dragon and I am the best knight of the king!"

"Slayed, Asher, not slaved," Mother says. But I don't know why because that's what I said. She is pulling potatoes out of the dirt and shaking them off. I will eat some of those for supper, probably.

"Oh, a butterfly!" yells my sister. I run to help her catch the butterfly. I bring my sword in case we find more dragons. I pretend she's the Princess and I'm the knight. Mother is the Queen and Father is the King.

My sister and me are the same amount tall and people say we have the same face. We have the same grey eyes, but she has Mother's brown hair and I have Father's blond hair. Ariana has white hair, too. But she isn't old.

I don't see the butterfly anymore. And Ariana is looking at something in the grass. I go to her and see what it is.

I hope it's a dragon, but it's just a half broke bird.

Ariana is talking to her friend, Sibley. Ariana says I have a friend, too, named Cinnamon, but Cinnamon doesn't talk to me and I can't see him. I wonder if Ariana is making up stories sometimes.

Mother picks potatoes, and Father points at carrots

and they jump into his brown sack. Sometimes he uses magic to make the carrots dance.

"Asher," Ariana says to me, "Sibley says Mother and Father could maybe fix the bird! Let's go!"

I run with Ariana to where Mother and Father are. I trip and fall. My pants rip in the knee and my sword breaks.

"Mother," Ariana asks, "will you fix this bird? Sibley says you can!"

Mother looks surprised and she leans backwards a little.

Father says, "Ariana, who is Sibley?"

Ariana tells him, "She is Mother's friend and my friend and Asher's friend in the forest. And this bird is broke."

Mother takes the bird from Ariana's hand.

"I broke my sword, Father! And also when I falled, I broke my trousers."

"Asher, you must be more careful," Father says. "Your mother will mend your trousers, but you'll have to find another sword."

Mother and Father are busy with Ariana and the broke bird that isn't even a dragon.

I go look for a new sword.

"Ariana never gets in trouble," I say. Maybe Cinnamon will hear me.

"They don't know how special you are." I am surprised to hear a toad talking to me. I didn't think Cinnamon was a toad.

"Animals only talk to Ariana," I say, forgetting about my sword.

"Come with me," the toad croaks. "I want to show you something." He hops off into the woods, and I follow him. He's not a dragon, but he is a talking toad.

CHAPTER THIRTEEN

Trapped Below

BELOW THE islands of Rhyme and Valorium, there are dozens of tunnels branching off in all directions. The islands themselves stand one hundred feet above sea level, so the tunnels go down quite deep. And although the caves have been dug by goblins and dwarves, they're not nearly as cramped as one might think. Even though a goblin stands only two feet tall, they build their caves high enough that a human of average height can stand almost upright. For one never knows when one will have to house a human.

Wooden beams provide support for the most central tunnels, to keep them from collapsing, which does happen from time to time.

Torches hang on the tunnel walls, every twenty feet or so, providing an eerie, flickering source of light. At random spots throughout the tunnels, there are chutes, indicating where a goblin might slide down into the underground. To a human walking through the forest, these goblin holes look like animal burrows and provide just a wide enough opening for a fat rabbit to slide through.

It had taken Grimblerod quite some time to create a hole large enough for a human child to enter.

WHEN HIS webbed feet hit the dirt, Grimblerod returns to his goblin form.

He is naked, as toads don't tend to wear clothes.

The boy slides down the hole behind him.

"Hello, have you seen a toad?" whispers the boy.

Grimblerod steps into the dirty trousers he'd left on the ground earlier in the day.

The boy looks up for the hole that he slid through to get down here. But the hole is not there.

"I have to go pick potatoes. I was just looking for my toad," he says.

Grimblerod grunts. He drags Asher by the arm several feet through the dark, damp tunnel using a candle to light their way. He points up above their heads to the potatoes planted in the earth above.

He hands the boy a dirty raw potato. Grimblerod picks one for himself and bites into it like an apple.

Grimblerod's sub-terrain home is not far from Lochlan and Gwendolyn's hut. The goblin lives in a tidy cave built beneath the pixie tree. The enormous yet intricate root system of the tree makes a mesmerizing ceiling. And the roots of pixie trees are a great source of magic for goblins and other such creatures.

Because he's been expecting to lure the child for quite some time, Grimblerod has prepared for his arrival. Knowing that humans grow taller than goblins, he has built an appropriately sized addition to his home where the boy will sleep. When he's not digging tunnels.

The goblin nudges Asher along the eerily lit passages to his home.

After a moment, they come to a small, rounded wooden door in the side of the tunnel. It is just tall enough for four-year-old Asher to fit through without having to bend over. Grimblerod turns the brass knob with his long crooked fingers, his overgrown fingernails scratching the wood.

Grimblerod uses the candle in his hand to light two torches that hang on the walls of his modest dwelling. Asher looks around at a cave that looks similar to his own hut, except there are no windows. Asher's eyes are drawn to the ceiling. A hundred long, bony fingers stretch out above him. He has never seen the roots of a tree from below before.

Grimblerod sets his candle down next to an ashtray and a bowl of acorns and mushrooms that sit atop a small sturdy table in the centre of the room. There is one wooden chair neatly tucked in underneath the table.

There is nothing else in the room except for small pile of straw in the corner covered with animal skins. Grimblerod's bed.

The goblin takes Asher by the arm and with his free hand pushes back a long, blueish-black curtain he has sewn with insect wings. It makes a gentle click clack sound as it sways back into place.

The room is a basic cave, about fifteen feet deep, with a few wooden beams for support. Torches hang on sconces on two of the walls. They are unlit, as there is plenty of sun coming in from the hole above.

Knowing also that humans need fresh air, Grimblerod has dug right up to the surface of the earth, leaving a two-foot wide hole at the top of the cave several feet past the pixie tree. Grimblerod has enchanted the opening to the hole where he will keep the boy, so Lochlan and Gwendolyn will see just a large patch of poison ivy when they walk by.

Grimblerod has covered the dirt floor with straw and has left some human items for the boy for comfort: a quill, a broken pot, and the skeleton of a rat.

When Grimblerod shoves Asher into his room the boy starts to cry.

He cries and cries. Grimblerod is afraid someone will hear the sound. He has not considered the fact that the child may scream.

Grimblerod pulls the smooth green stone from his pouch and holds it to the boy's neck. The child's eyes grow wide. The crying stops as a bright white light escapes his throat. Grimblerod holds out his hand to catch the light. A dazzling blue gem appears in his palm.

He looks at the green stone in his other hand, to see if it still has any power in it. The green colour has faded to grey, indicating that the stone's power has been depleted. This type of magic always comes with a cost, but Grimblerod has no choice. He will need to barter with the dwarves for another. For now, he tosses the green stone on the ground, then waddles off to his secret cavern where he will hide the blue gem made from the boy's voice.

The boy is left alone in the dark. Tears stream down his dirty cheeks leaving clean trails to the bottom of his chin. He silently cries himself to sleep.

Hours later, he wakes to loud voices calling his name above in the dark. He tries to scream and then he remembers he has no voice. He falls asleep again wondering what ever happened to that toad.

CHAPTER FOURTEEN

Ariana Worries

MOTHER SAYS, "We can't fix the bird's wing now, but we can take him home with us to help him get better."

"It will also help prevent making him a meal for a cat," I hear Father say.

Father pulls more potatoes out of the ground with his magic. Mother says, "We should bring these vegetables in and have lunch."

The garden is near the trees because Mother says some foods like all sun and some like shade. But we are still close to home. I can say the whole alphabet once, on a walk from home to the garden, so it is not far.

"Where did Asher go? He would like to help us with this bird!" I say.

"He probably went to the edge of the forest to find a new stick," says Father. "He knows not to go farther than where he can see us."

Father does not know that Asher breaks that rule every day. I always have to remind him to come back closer to where it's safe because we are twins and we are rare, and we must be careful always.

"I don't see him, Lochlan," Mother says. Her voice sounds worried.

Father stands up. "I'll go into the woods and get him," he says.

"Ariana," Mother says, "will you gather the bags of vegetables we've picked?" She is talking to me, but she is looking all around for Asher.

"Asher, dear, it's time for lunch!" she calls into the air.

I set the bird in a soft place on the grass. I look around

for hungry cats, and I don't see any.

"Sibley," I whisper. Sibley is always there when I whisper her name.

"Yes, Ariana. I will stay here with the bird," Sibley promises.

I smile and touch the bird very gently with my fingers.

I walk through the big garden and find the brown bags with vegetables inside. They are all my favourite vegetables: potatoes, beets, carrots, beans, and pumpkins. I am hungry, so I rub a carrot on the grass like Mother does and take a bite. It crunches and is delicious.

Mother calls Asher's name louder.

Father comes out of the woods. Asher is not with him. I try to hear what he says to Mother, but I am busy. I am dragging bags of vegetables to one place so Father can carry them home without forgetting one. Mother says Father could forget his own head it if it wasn't attached. But I don't think that's true.

I place all the bags together and fetch my bird from

Sibley.

"Where is Asher?" I ask. Sibley always has every answer to my questions. She's the one who told me why beets are purple and where stones come from.

"I wish I knew, dear. Cinnamon was called to the pixie tree around the same time we found the injured bird." Her face looks worried. "By the time he got back, Asher was nowhere to be seen."

"Will Cinnamon find Asher?"

"If Asher is within the kingdom, he will be found," Sibley says.

I do not ask what happens if Asher is not within the kingdom.

"Ariana," calls Mother. "Father is going to get some men to help find Asher." Sibley is invisible to Mother. Mother thinks it's odd that my imaginary friend and her childhood imaginary friend have the same name. She thinks she must have told me a story about having a friend named Sibley before and that's why I chose it. But that's silly because I didn't get to choose Sibley's name. Anyway, I think it's nice that we have the same watcher.

"We'll stay here in case Asher comes out of the woods from wherever he's hiding," Mother explains.

I look at Father. He is walking quickly toward our hut. He gets there faster than it would take me to finish saying the alphabet.

When Father comes back, there are more people than I can count along to help him. Mother takes me home to have lunch. I eat cheese and biscuits with honey, but Mother isn't hungry.

Father is still searching for Asher when it is time for bed that night.

I can't sleep without Asher beside me, and I am scared because I know he is scared where he is.

I don't say this to Mother because she is crying already.

Father searches for Asher every day.

Sibley tells me Cinnamon looks for Asher all day from the watching hole in the pixie tree, but so far he has not been able to spot him. Asher has vanished. That means disappeared.

Sibley says Cinnamon is broken-hearted because it's his fault. I wonder if broken-hearted is what I feel.

CHAPTER FIFTEEN

Raised in the Dark

ASHER ACHES for his family for many nights. He thinks of the stories his mother would tell as she tucked him into bed beside his sister each night. Of watching his father do magic. Of spending his days playing make-believe with Ariana.

The nights turn into more nights (for it always seems to be night underground) and Asher is now six years old. He can't tell if his memories are real. He begins to forget about his family and he believes now that Grimblerod is his father.

Grimblerod is not cruel to the boy, but he is unfeeling.

Every day, Asher digs tunnels for the goblin so that Grimblerod has more entry points to the surface. That is his job. He digs. All day long. With nothing but his bare hands.

Asher stops questioning the thoughts he sometimes has about green grass and blue skies.

Fresh air and birds.

A girl who looks just like him.

A soft mother and a strong father.

He spends his days digging, with Grimblerod watching his every move.

When he is taken to his room in Grimblerod's cave each night, he has nothing but the beetles and worms to keep him company. Even if he had someone to talk to, he has no voice to talk with. He falls asleep listening to the goblin grunt from the other end of the cave.

ARIANA'S NIMBLE fingers twist purple and yellow blossoms together.

Turning to Sibley she says, "Look how I twisted the heather into my crown!"

Sibley smiles. "Yes, Ariana. It is the most beautiful crown I have ever seen!"

Sibley loves seeing the child smile. After Asher's disappearance, things have been hard for Ariana. Her parents will never be the same. Lochlan no longer entertains Ariana with his silly magic tricks, and Gwendolyn's light has been extinguished by grief.

Sibley dreads the day that's bound to come. The day that Ariana stops seeing her. She is already six years old, the same age Gwendolyn was when she spoke with Sibley for the last time.

Ariana and Sibley are joined by a number of creatures: a chipmunk, a rabbit, a baby skunk, and a salamander. Nearby, Gwendolyn picks berries. Since Asher disappeared, she hasn't let Ariana out of her sight.

Lochlan and Gwendolyn are terrified she'll be snatched from them at any moment. With Asher gone, they aren't prepared to take any chances that Ariana's pure heart will be discovered. They can't bear to lose another child. They have been trying their hardest to conceal the enchanting glow and sweet nature that mark Ariana as a pure heart, but a soft light shines from the child like a beacon of goodness. So they do their best to keep Ariana away from others. From getting close to people. They rarely cross the footbridge to where the merchants are, and where the other islanders live.

"Sibley, this morning Mother and Father told me that Asher is not coming back. Does that mean he's not alive?" Ariana looks at Sibley with sad eyes.

Sibley sits on the little skunk's head and strokes his fluffy black and white fur. Sibley knows that since the fairies haven't been able to detect Asher, he's either underground, or in another realm. She chooses her words carefully.

"Ariana, I think your parents have given up hope that Asher is alive, but you mustn't do the same," she urges. "You are deeply connected to your brother, and if you feel he is alive, then he is alive. One day, I believe you will find him."

"I love it here with you, Sibley," Ariana says.

"I love it here with you too, my silver girl," Sibley

concurs, touching the silver hair on Ariana's head.

A breeze comes through off the ocean, causing a chorus of orange and yellow leaves to fall from the tree Ariana and Sibley are sitting under.

Ariana sits with her legs stretched out over the crisp leaves, enjoying the crunch they make when she moves her feet.

She stares at the knots at the base of the tree. Then at the feathery green moss and steely blue lichens that climb up the bark.

Ariana spots something glittery there within the grass.

She picks up the smooth piece of what appears to be glass, being careful not to cut herself. But this is not glass. It looks like a crystal or a jewel.

"Oh my," Sibley remarks. "You've found yourself quite a treasure, looks like!"

Ariana places her floral crown on her head and studies the crystal. It is magnificent.

"Do you think I can keep it?" Ariana questions the

fairy.

"Oh I can't see why not," she replies, "just ask your mother to be sure."

A smile stretches across Ariana's face. Sibley wishes she could see Gwendolyn smile this way. That Ariana could grow up in a happier shadow of herself. She wishes Gwendolyn and Lochlan could see that Ariana is growing sadder. That the goodness in her is not being fostered and these smiles are growing less frequent.

Sibley knows that soon Ariana will not see her. And after that day comes, she fears Ariana may never learn how to be happy.

CHAPTER SIXTEEN

Sibley Brings News to Ariana

THE WATER is cold on my toes but I don't care. I'm happy to be sitting on this smooth white rock with my feet in the ocean. It is me and my thoughts and the cry of the sea gulls.

It isn't easy to get away from Mother and Father. They demand to know where I am every single minute of my life. It feels like I am what they are living for, and all they care about is watching me at all times. Mother still cries over Asher. Father can't make her laugh like he did when I was a little girl. I have no friends because I can't risk anyone seeing what I really am.

I'm hours away from turning thirteen—I'm practically

an adult—and I'm not even allowed to go to the shore without my parents' permission. Father will be down to check on me any minute, I'm sure.

I watch the fishers coming in with their morning catches. They aren't much older than I am, and they are out there on the sea every day with only the breeze breathing down their necks.

The sun is dancing on the blue water, and I wonder what it would be like to be a mermaid at sea with all the freedom in the world. Instead, I'm like a fish in a net. Struggling to be free.

I pull a long strand of hair in front of my face and start twisting the streak of silver between two fingers. I do my best thinking that way.

Two moss farmers ride their horses along the water's edge, collecting Irish moss in giant rakes drawn by the animals. The air smells salty and fresh.

How I would love to climb onto one of those horses and ride off to a normal life, out from under their thumbs. I love them so much, but I'm ready to be treated like an adult and to start a new life somewhere far away.

"Don't say that, my dear."

Did I say that out loud? No. I hadn't.

"Who said that?" I ask, scanning the area for the source of the voice.

"Don't you remember me, my dear Ariana? It's me, Sibley."

A tiny fairy with pale blue hair sits on the rock next to me. Her wings are sparkling. They look like glass.

I haven't thought of Sibley for years.

"Sibley?"

She smiles at me. She reminds me of Mother. I never noticed that when I was little.

"It's been so long, Sibley! We had so much fun together! I can't believe it's you!"

"I feared you would have forgotten about me like your mother did," says Sibley.

"Mother and Father have been so sad, Sibley. I remember when I was little, Mother would get upset at the mention of your name. I had to stop talking about you, so eventually I stopped thinking about you. But I've never forgotten you."

"I've always been here, Ariana. Humans usually see us fairies as fragments of light. Have you ever noticed flashes or twinkles at times when you've been sad?" Sibley asks.

"That was you? I've always thought I was seeing things, it happens so quickly!"

"Humans aren't able to see us. But you pure hearts are so trusting, especially as children, that you generally can. Like you and your mother. Gwendolyn had to try very hard to forget me," Sibley says. "But your father, he was assigned a watcher when he was a baby and he never had any idea."

I think about times when I was young, after Asher left, and how Sibley was the only friend I had. I loved her fiercely. She was my whole world, especially when Mother and Father became detached.

"Mother and Father were so much fun when Asher

and I were little," I say. "Father was always using his magic to make us laugh, and Mother had such stories about pixies and fairies."

Sibley smiles. "Gwendolyn remembered me and the pixies on some level. Many of those stories were probably true and she didn't even know!"

"Sibley, will things ever be the same as they once were?"

"I'm afraid I don't know, dear," admits Sibley.

"Almost all of Mother's light has gone out since Asher died, and Father is just so sad all of the time."

"Does your father practice any magic?" Sibley asks.

"No. I haven't seen him do so much as a simple trick since Asher left," I reply.

Sibley frowns. "Not even to make a pot of tea? He did that the morning you were born, you know. I recall thinking, how lazy! But it was rather endearing."

I try to remember the last time I saw Father use his magic when my thought is interrupted by Sibley's voice.

"What do you remember about the day Asher left, Ariana?"

"I remember that it was my fault. Mother and Father were fussing over me and a broken-winged bird. If it weren't for me, Asher never would have gone missing. He never would have died."

I'm surprised by how much better I feel after even just thinking those thoughts to another set of ears.

"Oh dear, if it was anyone's fault, it was mine. I was the one who told you that day to bring the bird to your parents. Don't you remember?" whispers Sibley.

I nod. But I don't feel any better.

"All that was a long time ago, Ariana, and there's nothing to be gained by blaming yourself. It was not your fault. It hurts me that you're so sad." Sibley pauses and says, "Dear, there's something you need to know."

"What is it?" Sibley's tiny blue eyebrows are drawn in to her nose. She looks like she's about to say something important.

"I've been hesitant to tell you, but I think you are old

enough now to know," Sibley begins.

I wait for her to speak again.

"Asher is alive."

"What do you mean, *alive?*"

I've always felt like Asher was still alive. I have felt it in my heart, the same heart that is pounding loudly right now.

"Child, you don't seem as shocked as I expected you would be."

"Sibley, I've always felt he was still alive, that we were still connected. But talking about Asher has always made Mother and Father so sad that I forced myself long ago to accept he was dead. Despite my gut feelings."

"Never doubt your instincts, dear. Never."

"But Sibley, why haven't you told me before? Why haven't you told Mother?"

"Because she refuses to see me or hear me, Ariana. I have tried many times to speak to her, but as you say, her light has faded."

"Where is he, Sibley?"

"He was taken and hidden somewhere, Ariana. I don't know where. But Calla feels that he is now in danger. We don't know how much longer he has, but you are his only hope."

"Who's Calla?" I ask.

"She is the ruler of the fairy realm," Sibley explains.

"How can I be Asher's only hope? What do I have to do with this?"

"You are both so connected, if anyone is going to find him, it will be you," Sibley says.

"Where do we start?" I ask.

"I don't know, Ariana. Oh!" Sibley squeaks, spotting something behind me.

"What is it?" I turn and see that Father is coming down to the shore.

"We will talk later, dear." And, in a flash of blue light, Sibley is gone.

CHAPTER SEVENTEEN

Asher's Dream

I STAND in the middle of an open field. The sun has set and the sky is bruised purple and grey.

Is this real?

Wolves howl from someplace nearby. I try to move, but I am planted here in one place.

Am I dreaming?

A girl walks over to me. She is my age. She calls out, "Asher!" It's been so long since I've heard my name.

I try to call to her, but when I open my mouth, there

is no sound.

A voice comes from nowhere. "Asher, don't you remember your sister?"

"You have a twin," the voice declares.

The ground beneath me rumbles. Cracks appear in the grass. I lose my balance. Between me and the girl, monstrous green vines thrust from the earth, wide as tree trunks. They grow all around the girl, trapping her in a prison of vines, twisting together like fingers. She is silent. She does not call out. Can she see me?

When the vines reach the height of me, they begin to snap as they sprout enormous thorns.

A woman appears beside me.

I have to crane my neck to see her face. The top of my head is level with her waist. She looks familiar. She is beautiful.

She cannot see me. She is here but she is somewhere else.

A man appears. He is angry, and he storms at the

woman. I am still unable to move.

They are chanting strange words.

"Exterminant montem!" The words she throws at the man send him reeling backward.

He aims his hands at her, shouting, "Lapidem!" A beam of light hits the woman in the chest, breaking the pendant that hangs around her neck.

The man disappears.

The woman turns to stone.

I sense that I am being shown this for a reason. I am supposed to pay attention.

Silence. The vines have stopped growing. The girl is no longer there.

I hear that voice again. The one that told me I have a sister. It sounds sad. "The wizard who locked me in this stone prison many years before you were born is the monster who has stolen your childhood and the lives of countless others. The last spell I cast was meant to protect the world from him and his evil, but he was too strong for me to kill."

"I was only able to banish him from this place. I know not what dark magic he has been doing with the hearts, souls, and bones the children he has killed, but, with your help, I can stop him."

My heart pounds in my ears.

"Asher, only the power of you and your sister can release me so that I can defeat Larque. You two are of my blood and the power of three will end him and will prevent the suffering of parents across the land."

I am back in my cave. But the voice continues to speak to me.

"You must find Ariana. You each hold a missing piece of the pendant. Bring them to my monument. This must happen while you both still have the innocence of your childhood. This must happen before your thirteenth birthday."

I don't understand.

"You, sweet child, do not belong beneath the surface of the earth. You have been deprived of sunshine and fresh air. Of exercise and knowledge of the human experience. Of the love of your parents. If you do not soon escape your prison, my dear boy, you will die."

I wake up sweating. I lift my face from the cold floor and grope in the dark for the candle that sits in the dirt beside the clay pot I eat from.

I light the candle and shine its light on the wall in front of me. There are thousands of short lines carved in the dirt. One for each day I've been here.

What is a thirteenth birthday?

I reach for the broken piece of crystal that I found one day years ago while I was digging for Grimblerod. It always makes me feel better to hold it.

I hold the crystal in my hand and listen to the goblin snore. I try to remember Ariana. Then I fall back to sleep.

CHAPTER EIGHTEEN

Ariana is Warned

I WAKE from a deep sleep.

Mother and Father snore softly on the other side of the hut. I open my eyes. A pair of eyes look back at me.

I am stiff. Frozen. I can't breathe.

He wears a black hood. I can't see his face, but I see that his skin looks half-melted off his bones.

My heart beats fast.

I feel the straw poke me beneath my blanket, so I know I'm not dreaming.

"Ariana," he says as he hovers above me. He knows my name.

"Sibley knows not what she says. You mustn't listen to her for she has been influenced by the witch, Elora. Elora is not what she seems. She may have gotten to your brother already. You must not seek Asher out. If you do, an evil will be unleashed on mankind. An evil like nothing ever seen before."

And just as quickly as it appeared, the vision is gone.

Elora. The good witch. My ancestor. The one who led Mother and Father to move to this safe village by the sea so that we would all be untouched by evil.

So much for that.

Who was that man? Was it the dark wizard that Elora warned Father of all those years ago?

You were mesmerized, Ariana, I tell myself. *Elora has been advising your family for many years. He is trying to trick you, as evil ones do. You must find Asher, as Sibley says.*

I get up from my sleeping mat and pull on my boots. I

have to go to the ocean so I can think. Mother and Father will be furious, but judging by the high position of the moon, I will be back before they wake.

Before I leave, I check the pocket of my nightgown for the piece of crystal I found when I was a little girl. I always had this foolish idea that it would keep me safe. But, who knows? Maybe it's been working.

I quietly creep outside, and I see Sibley's wings twinkle in the night.

"Sibley! I'm so happy to see you," I say. "But what are you doing here?"

"You were thinking of me, Ariana. You were hoping I would come!" Sibley says. She is right.

The wet grass soaks my ankles as I walk to the shore with my old friend.

"How are we going to find Asher?"

"I've been watching you every day of your life, dear Ariana," she says. "You have no idea how powerful you are, do you?"

"I don't feel powerful, Sibley," I say.

"Well, you are. And the sooner you become open to the magic inside of you, the sooner I believe you will be able to lead us to Asher."

"Sibley, I had a vision tonight," I say. "I think it was the dark wizard, but it did not feel evil. I should have been more afraid than I was."

We've almost reached the edge of the tall rocky cliff, and I carefully lower myself down without tripping over the bottom of my long nightgown.

"You must trust your instincts, Ariana," Sibley reasons. "They will not mislead you."

"But Sibley," I say, "the man told me not to listen to you. That I am not to search for Asher. What am I to do? Should I ask Father and Mother?"

"I expect if this was a matter your parents could fix they would be the ones having these visitations," says Sibley.

"Do you know who the man could have been?" I ask her.

"I suspect it was Larque," Sibley says.

The tide is low. I walk to where the tidal pools sparkle beneath the light of the full moon. "Who is Larque?" I ask.

I sit down and toss a small pebble into the water creating a succession of ripples on the surface. Sibley doesn't speak. She is looking at the water.

Then I see it. There is a beautiful face looking up at me from the pool. It can only be Elora. I jump back, startled.

"My child," she says to me, "you were visited in your sleep by the dark one. He is growing stronger. He has a grand plan to create a special magic race, ridding the planet of all living things to do so. I can stop him, but I need your help. You must get to your brother because only you two together can release me. We must stop him from ripping these children from their mothers and fathers. "

The image changes from one of Elora's face to that of a boy my age. He looks so much like me... *could it be?*

"Asher! Sibley, it's Asher!" I cry out.

I study the image in the water. Asher is sleeping on the dirt. It is so dark.

"Where is he?"

"Go to the pixie tree," commands Elora.

Another ripple in the water and the image changes to the tall old tree at the centre of the village. "Beyond the stream that runs past that tree, there is a patch of what appears to be poison ivy. That is an illusion to stop humans from finding the opening to the cave where your brother sleeps."

"You must find him before you turn thirteen, Ariana," Elora continues. "After your thirteenth birthday, your powers will weaken with the loss of your childhood innocence. You will be unable to free me."

"Sibley, I turn thirteen at midnight!"

But Sibley is already racing for the pixie tree.

There is no time to worry about what will happen when Mother and Father wake up and find me gone. Or about the fact that I'm wearing only a nightgown.

CHAPTER NINETEEN

Found

"I ALWAYS imagined this was a pixie tree!" I say to Sibley.

"Yes, Ariana," Sibley tells me. "It is a grand old tree, isn't it? Remember how we used to sit here and talk for hours and hours?"

I smile at the memory. But we have no time to reminisce.

"Elora said the poison ivy patch is past this stream," I say. I run to the very place where the stream begins. "It must be here somewhere."

"Wait for me!" I hear a tiny voice I don't recognize.

"Cinnamon!" Sibley says. "Come, help us! You remember Ariana?"

"Of course!" says Cinnamon. "I can't tell you how sorry I am, Ariana," he says. "I have not stopped looking for your brother, even after all these years. But I hear we have a location on him now! I'm here to help."

I don't remember Cinnamon, but I will search my memory later.

"Let's go," I say. "There's no time or need for placing blame."

Sibley kneels down in the grass. "It is very difficult to spot poison ivy in the dark," she says. "And you certainly don't want to find the patch that isn't enchanted, you with your delicate human skin!"

"Could that be it?" Cinnamon points to a patch of tall menacing poison ivy leaves.

"Oh I think it could be!" Sibley flies down to the plant.

"No," Cinnamon says. "Let me do this. Please."

Sibley flits out of the way.

While Cinnamon pokes around the grass, I have an odd feeling. "Sibley," I say.

"Yes, dear?"

"Why did Elora wait until now to tell us where Asher is?"

"I was thinking that same thing, Ariana. She must have had reason. Perhaps she just found out herself where he was taken. Perhaps Larque's magic is weakening. All that matters is that we now know where to look."

I MUST be seeing things. Is that a small hand?

I study my own hand for comparison.

Because the moon is full, Grimblerod is above the surface. On full-moon nights the goblin stays out until daybreak. It is quiet without the sound of Grimblerod's snoring.

I can't sleep after that nightmare I had earlier.

I shake my head and close my eyes before opening them again. But that definitely is a tiny hand reaching down into this hole.

I try to call out, to let the owner of the hand know that I'm down here, but there is no use.

I can't speak.

"Ariana, I think this is the spot," I hear a voice say from above.

A tiny winged creature flies down into the hole.

I cower. What if this creature is here to harm me?

I don't think it's human, for the creature is much smaller than I am. And it certainly isn't a goblin.

CINNAMON CRIES out at the sight of him.

He is not much more than a pile of bones in a filthy bag of skin!

the fairy thinks.

The smell coming from the boy is overwhelming.

Asher is encased in a thick layer of dirt. It looks like he has not had a bath for a very long time—possibly since he went missing. His hair is the same length as his sister's, hanging down almost to his bottom.

His pale face is gaunt, and Cinnamon can count the ribs that show above the animal skin that he wears around his waist.

How he must have suffered! Surely, he isn't strong enough to help Ariana!

A face looks down from above, and Asher's own lights up. He recognizes her from the dream he had earlier that night.

"Asher," she whispers. "Asher, is it really you?"

He nods.

Ariana tries to jump down to her brother, but Sibley reaches out to stop her.

"No, Ariana, there is a risk that Asher's captor is still down there," Sibley says. "Cinnamon," she calls out, "are you and Asher down there alone?"

Cinnamon shrugs. "I have no idea," he whispers.

Ariana reaches into the hole, offering her brother her hand, but he is out of her reach.

Cinnamon crouches down and holds on to Asher's ankles. He starts to fly with all his might, lifting the boy up off the ground high enough for him to reach Ariana. Ariana hoists him up out of his cave.

Asher takes his first breath of fresh air in over eight years. He coughs.

"Slow down, dear boy," says Cinnamon, flying out of the hole. "Breathe slowly. There, that's better."

Tears spring to Ariana's eyes as she throws her arms around her brother. He recoils from her touch.

"Asher?" Ariana reaches out for her brother.

"It's ok, Ariana," soothes Sibley. "Remember, your brother has not seen another human since he last saw

you over eight years ago. He's bound to be a little timid.
"

"Asher, I can't believe it's really you! Mother and Father won't believe it! We thought you were dead." Ariana studies her brother's face. Fat tears roll down her cheeks.

Should I trust the winged things and the girl? Asher wonders.

The dream he had earlier makes him think he should.

But I'm afraid. Asher grasps tightly to the shard of crystal—the only thing in the world he has that is his.

"Asher, I can't wait to get you home to Mother and Father, but there's something you and I need to do, first. It's a bit of a long story, but you and I turn thirteen in a couple of hours and before that happens, we need to free Elora from stone."

Asher remembers the message from his dream. He nods to let her know he understands.

Before Asher and Ariana can decide what to do next, a vision of Elora appears in front of them.

"Well done, children," she purrs. "You have made me proud."

"Oh, my sweet boy," Elora says gently to Asher. "Let's get you cleaned up."

A few flashes of light and Asher's hair is trimmed neat and tidy below his ear lobes, his skin is clean, and he is wearing a fresh tunic and trousers.

"Go, now, children, go to the statue. Help save me so I can defeat the dark one."

LARQUE STARES into the flame of his fire. He sees that Ariana and Asher have found each other. He watches as the siblings now race to the statue of Elora in the centre of Rhyme.

I must stop them.

CHAPTER TWENTY

To the Statue

ARIANA RUNS, leading Asher past the pixie tree, through a small stand of trees.

A branch comes out of nowhere and snaps Asher hard in the face. The welt on his cheek stings terribly. He wishes he could tell Ariana to slow down while he catches his breath.

"Crispy crickets!" Cinnamon shouts. He had been flying ahead of Asher when he felt a jolt. Watchers feel whatever pain is inflicted on their humans, so now his cheek was stinging. "Sorry about that, Ash! I'm rusty with this watching business."

Asher shakes it off and nods.

Up ahead, Ariana has almost reached the wooden footbridge that crosses the stream. Sibley is flying behind her.

It feels so big outside, Asher thinks. His legs are having a difficult time carrying him. Those years underground have weakened his muscles.

Asher has a memory then, of that day in the garden so long ago. The day he wandered into the forest by himself and followed a cunning toad down a hole.

A chill runs down his spine as he runs to catch up to his sister. He can make out the shape of a statue on the other side of the stream.

A tree root leaps out of the ground and throws itself in front of Ariana, tripping her. She flies across the ground, landing on her face. Sibley puts her hand to her own face, which now feels like she's had a fall.

Asher catches up to his sister and reaches out his hand, helping her to her feet.

"I wonder what that was?" Ariana asks, but she

doesn't wait for anyone to answer before she's off running again.

Asher exhales deeply and races after her.

When they arrive at the statue, they see Sibley there waiting for them.

As Ariana stops to catch her breath, she feels something bump her head.

"Ouch!" she cries, ducking.

Asher feels something hit his head, too.

Large brown bats, the size of rabbits, dive at Ariana and Asher. The twins can hear wings flapping and a hissing sound coming from the creatures' throats.

Within seconds, the air is thick with bats. Sibley and Cinnamon take cover beneath a toadstool on the ground. Asher and Ariana kneel on the cold, damp grass and cover their heads from the assault.

"Sibley! Why are we not able to protect them?" Cinnamon cries as the giant bats swoop around Ariana and Asher.

"I don't know, Cinnamon," Sibley says. "But something is happening. There must be magic behind these creatures. Magic stronger than us."

Ariana has never before encountered an animal that has tried to harm her. *Something is happening*, she thinks, swatting yet another bat away as it nips her shoulder. *Is someone... or something after us?*

She shakes off the thought and reaches for her brother's hand. As soon as her hand clasps around Asher's, the twins feel a jolt of electricity and there is a flicker of blue light.

The twins stare at their hands for a moment and then they notice the sound has faded. The bats are gone.

Ariana lets go of Asher's hand and rises. "What was that?" she asks the fairies, who emerge from beneath the red cap of the toadstool.

"I don't know, Ariana." Sibley looks as confused as the twins.

"Well, we don't have time to figure it out now. Asher, get up, let's go!" Ariana instructs her brother.

THEY AREN'T making this easy, thinks Larque, watching the events unfold in the smoke of his enchanted fire.

It is almost midnight.

The statue of Elora is steps away.

"COME ON, Asher!" Ariana runs to the statue and reaches behind for Asher who is unable to run as well as her.

When Ariana turns back around, she sees that an ogre has appeared in front of Elora's monument.

The rotten stench coming from him is like nothing Asher or Ariana have had the displeasure of smelling before. His face is wider than a dinner plate.

He stands about eight feet high and he is holding a wooden club in one hand. Pale blue skin stretches across his muscular frame. Patches of moss have sprouted around his neck, armpits, and feet.

The beast opens his mouth and roars exposing rows of brown teeth coated with green algae. Black bits of who-knows-what are jammed in between them.

His giant feet stomp closer to Ariana and Asher. He picks up the club in his hand and raises it in the air. "Look out, Asher!" Ariana cries.

The twins jump back out of the monster's way, terrified.

"Sibley, help!" Ariana yells. But she receives no reply because Sibley is flying around the ogre's head.

"Cinnamon, watch the children from your position on the ground," orders Sibley. "I'll see if I can distract him and get him away from the monument!"

"It's too dangerous, Sibley!" Cinnamon yells.

"I have no choice!" Sibley calls back. "He's trying to separate Ariana and Asher, and we can't let that happen!"

The ogre swings the club through the air, high above his head.

"Sibley, look out!" hollers Cinnamon.

Sibley looks up to see the club directly above her. She buzzes left and then right. But the magic in the ogre is weakening her. She is disoriented. The ogre's club comes down hard on the back of her head, and she falls to the ground.

Ariana screams and runs to Sibley.

The beast drops the club and kneels down to get it.

"Sibley! Sibley!" Ariana cries. But Sibley's wings have stopped sparkling. She is motionless. Cinnamon flies down and sits beside her.

This ogre is not playing games. With his club back in one hand, he picks Ariana up off the ground with the other and throws her as easily as if she were a potato. She lands back on the other side of the stream.

Sibley, Sibley, help!

But Sibley does not come.

Ariana is dizzy and her ankle is sore, but not too sore

for her to run. She picks herself up and sprints back to her brother. The ogre now holds Asher above his head, about to toss him like he had Ariana.

Cinnamon, trying to distract the ogre, darts back and forth at the monster's nose. The ogre drops his club to the ground and uses his hand to try and grab the fairy.

All those years I spent wishing I was normal, thinks Ariana. *I would give anything to have magical powers right about now.* Her silver hair starts to glow.

She thinks of all the babies who have died or have been stolen from their families, all because of Larque.

He has to be stopped!

"Cinnamon, we're running out of time—it must be almost midnight!" Ariana yells.

I must be brave. Ariana takes a deep breath and starts toward the ogre.

"Hang on, Cinnamon! I'm coming!" Ariana yells.

"Ariana! I can't hold him much longer..."

Ariana races toward the ogre, still not quite sure of what she'll do when she gets there. Then she hears a new voice.

"Ariana, wait! We're here to help!" Fidget bounces up into Ariana's hand and Wink jumps onto her shoulder.

Ariana doesn't recognize the creatures. She doesn't know who they are or how they knew about the ogre, but there's no time for questions now. She keeps running in the direction of the ogre. "We need to stop him!"

"Wink, go help Cinnamon and create a distraction!" squeaks Fidget, aiming for the ogre's feet. "I know just what to do!"

Wink buzzes up in front of the beast's face. "Hey, ogre, come and get me!" he yells.

Ariana watches as Fidget jumps to the ogre's feet and starts to tie the laces of his boots together .

Infuriated (ogres are known for having very little patience), the monster heaves himself at the pixie. With Wink just within his reach, he trips over his laces and falls flat on his face with a big thud, hitting his head on a large stone.

Cinnamon catches Asher before the ogre falls, and he sets him down gently.

When Ariana sees that her brother is all right and that Cinnamon is with him, she rushes to Sibley. She sobs at the sight of the lifeless fairy.

Ariana feels Asher's arm around her. Cinnamon kneels at her side.

"Here, grab this." Wink tosses a rope end to Fidget.

"Where did you get this?" squeaks Fidget. She takes the rope and runs across the ogre's back to his hand.

"This is no time to discuss logistics!" Wink runs over to her with the other end of the rope.

The two pixies, used to tying human hair in knots while they sleep, have never dealt with a creature of this size before.

"Are you sure this will work?" screeches Fidget.

"No, but do you have any ideas?" asks Wink.

Fidget and Wink run back and forth with the rope, tying the ogre's hands and feet together.

"Hey, now can you tell me where you got the never-ending length of rope, Wink?"

"Do we really need to discuss that at this very moment?" cries Wink, trying to tighten a knot that could restrain a giant monster.

"You can get back to me," says Fidget.

LARQUE IS shocked. He has truly underestimated the children. He was sure his ogre would have sent them off.

I am left with no other options. I must go to Lochlan.

SIBLEY ISN'T breathing.

I think we can fix her, Asher thinks.

Ariana looks at her brother and nods.

The twins stare at each other.

I can hear what you think, Ariana communicates to her brother.

And I you, he thinks in response.

Asher carefully lifts Sibley's tiny body from the grass. With the fairy laying on his palm, he extends his hands to his sister. She gently places her hands on his. Fidget, Wink, and Cinnamon watch.

The twins wait for that same buzzing that had happened before, with the bats.

Nothing's happening, Ariana.

I know, Brother. But I can't lose her. I can't.

A tear rolls down her cheek. It falls on Sibley's wing.

Now they feel that same buzzing they felt before. Sibley's wings start to sparkle and the colour returns to her body.

Asher smiles.

"Sibley? Can you hear me?" Ariana asks.

"Oh yes, dear, but please don't speak so loudly. My poor head." Sibley touches the place where the ogre's club made contact.

Ariana wipes her tears. "I'm so glad you're ok!"

"Yes!" Fidget and Wink squeal, giving Cinnamon high fives.

"What happened here, then? When did you two arrive?" Sibley asks, looking down at the ogre and then at the pixies.

"Well, it was all quite exciting!" Fidget says proudly. "As luck would have it, I was watching through the pixie tree and saw that you needed help. Let me tell you about how Wink and I saved the day—"

"Asher and Ariana!" Cinnamon interrupts, gesturing to the statue. "It's time!"

CHAPTER TWENTY-ONE

Another One Gone

"GWENDOLYN, WHERE could she be?" cries Lochlan when he discovers Ariana is not in her bed.

"Lochlan, have we lost both of them?" Gwendolyn sobs.

Before Lochlan can answer his wife, an apparition appears in the hut. A man in a black hood.

Lochlan has been visited in his dreams many times since he was a child, but he's never experienced a vision like this.

"Lochlan, the witch has tricked Ariana into thinking

she can save the kingdom from darkness. You must destroy the statue of Elora and prevent her from entering our realm."

The vision grows blurry.

"Elora has the child convinced that I must be destroyed. But if Ariana does what she has been lured to do, the witch will kill her, along with you and Gwendolyn and everyone she can find within reach. She is from the devil and wants to destroy humankind to start a new race, populating the planet with dark demons and evil magicians.

Gwendolyn gasps.

"The last thing Elora did before I cast her to stone, in an effort to stop her evil plan, was to banish me to the mountains on the island of Valorium. I cannot go to Rhyme, or else I would have destroyed the statue myself, long ago."

"Elora is of my blood," Lochlan fumes. "She is our protector! She is goodness and light. I don't believe you. You are the evil one. It is you who is responsible for the loss of my boy!" Lochlan's face is red. His heart is beating faster and faster. "You are trying to fool me."

"Lochlan, you must believe me. It is Elora who is evil. She must be destroyed."

"Why have you not come before?" Gwendolyn questions the apparition.

"I have not needed to," explains Larque.

"I will not destroy the statue. You're trying to deceive me!" Lochlan states.

And without waiting for the vision to respond, Lochlan takes his wife's hand and races out into the night.

CHAPTER TWENTY-TWO

Freeing Elora

"YOU HAVE pleased me greatly, children." Elora's voice acknowledges Asher and Ariana as they stand in front of her statue.

The siblings smile.

She's so tall, Ariana thinks. *She looks taller than Father!*

"Asher, the crystal in your hand," urges Elora, "and the crystal in your pocket, Ariana. Those are the broken pieces of my pendant. You two together must hold the crystals and place them on my chest, next to the other shard that hangs around the statue's neck."

Ariana pulls the shard of crystal from her pocket. Asher holds out his palm.

Where did you get that? Ariana thinks, looking at the crystal in Asher's hand.

I'll explain later.

Ariana and Asher take their crystals and approach the statue. They raise the pieces up and are about to touch them to the pendant on the statue when the sound of running feet and voices distracts them. They look up and see Lochlan and Gwendolyn racing toward them.

"Ariana, wait!" Lochlan yells.

Asher turns and looks into the faces of his parents.

Lochlan and Gwendolyn stop running. They both look as though they've seen a ghost. "Asher?" Lochlan cries as he and Gwendolyn slowly approach the boy. "How? Is it really you?" He pulls Asher into his arms. He then holds him out at arm's length to get a look at him.

Asher smiles.

"My Asher!" Gwendolyn cries. "My Asher, where have you been all this time?"

When Asher sees his mother cry, tears roll down his own face as well. She pulls him into a tight hug.

"Mother, Father, he can't speak," Ariana says. "I haven't learned why yet, but I will. I can communicate with him, but there's no time to tell you more. We are so close now—we must free Elora and lift the curse."

A concerned look washes over Lochlan's face.

Larque's words swirl in Lochlan's head. No, it couldn't be possible that Elora was the dark one. Could it be? He was so sure that Larque was trying to deceive him back at his hut. But, now, faced with what his children—both his children!—were about to do, he begins to have doubts.

Has she manipulated the children with her beauty?

"Get those thoughts out of your head, grandson," Elora's voice cautions him. "He is trying to trick you. It is he who has stolen the souls of so many children through the years. It is he who took your brother and your son from you. He will not stop until he spreads his misery to all corners of the Earth!"

"Lochlan," urges Gwendolyn, "this doesn't feel right to me. The energy coming from Elora. It feels... dark."

Lochlan hears Larque's words over and over in his head. His grimoire has always told him what to do, but there is no time to consult it.

Asher and Ariana look at each other. They touch their crystals together.

"Don't do anything yet, children!" Gwendolyn yells.

She is holding Lochlan's arm. "Lochlan," she says, "I think Larque was telling the truth. We must listen to him."

Lochlan nods slowly and starts to speak when Gwendolyn's grip on his arm tightens.

"Lochlan!" she yells. "Look at Ariana's hair!"

Ariana reaches for the silver in her hair, but it's gone.

"Mother, what's happening to me?" Ariana yells.

"Remember, Loch," Gwendolyn says with panic in her voice, "when Elora came to you in a vision and led us to Rhyme? What if she lured us here with wicked intentions?"

"Ariana!" Lochlan yells. "Asher! Wait! You mustn't! Elora is not what she seems!"

"Children, quick!" cries Elora. "Larque has manipulated your parents. Hurry!"

With a nod, Ariana and Asher hold the crystals up to the stone pendant of the statue.

"No!" Gwendolyn cries, reaching for Ariana and Asher.

The ground shakes. The stone figure of Elora begins to crack.

A great moan comes from deep within Elora, louder than a crack of thunder. The twins cover their ears. Gwendolyn and Lochlan throw their arms around Ariana and Asher. Sibley, Cinnamon, Fidget, and Wink are at their feet.

Colours drift across the starry night sky. Pink, green,

and yellow. Aurora Borealis adding to the drama of the night's events.

The statue crumbles and Elora rises from the earth. She stands at least seven feet tall, but she continues to grow taller. And taller. Against a background of northern lights.

A great cackle comes from her throat. "Fooooools!"

"Oh Asher," Ariana cries, "what have we done?"

CHAPTER TWENTY-THREE

The Battle

"WHAT HAVE we done?" Ariana screams again.

The beautiful Elora is no more. She's been transformed into a demon, a monster. Ariana grabs hold of Asher and they watch the hideous creature rise up into the colourful night sky.

Her skin is grey. She appears to be thousands of years old.

Her fingers are topped with razor-sharp claws.

She rises high above Ariana and Asher's heads, and she grows larger and larger. She is climbing in a cloud of blue mist.

"Let's get out of here!" Fidget yells, racing for the pixie tree. Wink follows close behind, but Sibley and Cinnamon stay by Asher and Ariana's side.

"You are all mine. ALL of you, MINE!" Elora screams, her form swirling against the ever-changing night sky, its black canvas being painted by the northern lights.

"Ilsegoria, magniforia, meldinerium. Ilsegoria, magniforia, meldinerium..." she chants.

Pained screams and tortured moans come from all directions.

A cloud of vapour appears next to Lochlan. It slowly materializes into the shape of a man.

"What are you doing here?" Lochlan shouts. It is Larque.

"I thought you were unable to step foot on the island!" Lochlan says.

"I don't understand myself," says Larque. "But it

seems as though Elora being released has also released me."

"I'm afraid we were wrong about Elora. And possibly about you," admits Lochlan.

"What is she doing?" Gwendolyn screams, her voice getting lost amid all the other cries. She holds Asher and Ariana close. "What is she chanting?"

"She is calling on the Jagwa, an ancient race of demons that was destroyed centuries ago," Larque explains. "These creatures must not be unleashed. If humans look at them, their hearts stop." Larque extends his hand to Asher and Ariana. "You must trust me," he says.

We've trusted before, Sister, and look where it's gotten us! Ariana nods in agreement with her brother. "Father, Mother, I'm scared!" she cries. "What are we to do?"

The moans and screams grow louder as black shapes rise from the earth, creating hundreds of human-like forms in the night sky.

Larque grabs Asher and Ariana. He puts their hands to his. A great beam of light radiates from their palms.

Elora laughs. "What are you fools trying to do?"

One of the Jagwa demons flies from the sky and intercepts, exploding in the beam emitting from their hands.

"Larque," she says, "you are even more pathetic than I remember. You are not strong enough to defeat me."

Asher and Ariana, still holding hands, begin to shake.

I hope he has a plan, thinks Asher.

"Helginorium, malniforium, perkadonium..." Larque chants, his eyes closed.

Elora stops laughing and hurls a piece of rock from the crumbled statue at Asher and Ariana.

The twins jump out of the way. Gwendolyn and Lochlan rush to them. When they see the children are not harmed, they look over at Larque. He opens his eyes, nods at them. Lochlan and Gwendolyn help the twins to their feet.

Asher and Ariana hold hands and walk to Larque

once more, putting their hands on his.

"Helginorium, malniforium, perkadonium…" Larque chants again.

Ariana chants with Larque. Somehow, she knows the words.

"It is time for me to collect my souls, Larque," Elora's voice rumbles in the night.

The earth shakes and groans.

"What's happening?" Gwendolyn cries.

"You," Elora points at Asher. "I wish to start my collection with you."

"No!" Gwendolyn screams and covers Asher with her body.

Giant green vines break through the ground. Enormous tendrils twist around Asher's feet like the arms of a sinister octopus. The vine grabs him and hurls him up into the air to the witch, breaking his grip on his sister's hand.

Just like in my dream! he thinks.

Ariana screams. Cinnamon flies up with Asher.

Another vine twists around the ankles of Larque. And then one takes Lochlan.

They are both hurled up into the air by the vines.

Ariana, Gwendolyn, and Sibley watch in horror.

A cloud of black swirls around Larque, Lochlan, and Asher. They look like flies being spun into a spider's web.

"I now have two descendants and the powerful Larque," Elora smiles. "Three hearts to start my work. All of that magic blood!" Elora swirls and cackles in the night.

"JAGWA!" she screams. "Kill them!"

The black figures of the Jagwa become clearer. The hideous, skinless creatures with horns and claws swoop in over Larque, Lochlan, and Asher.

"DON'T LOOK AT THEM!" screams Larque into the night.

Gwendolyn shields Ariana's eyes from the Jagwa demons.

"Mother!" Ariana shouts. "Why can't Father and Larque use their magic against her?"

"I don't know, Ariana." Gwendolyn is crying. She squeezes her arms around Ariana. "They're powerless!"

"It is up to you," Ariana suddenly hears Sibley say. "It is up to you and your mother, Ariana."

Gwendolyn looks at Ariana's shoulder. "Did you just see a blue light, Ariana?" she asks.

"Mother, take my hand!" Ariana says.

Sibley sits in Gwendolyn's palm. Her wings glow. Out of the corner of Ariana's eye, she sees her streak has started glowing, too.

Gwendolyn smiles as she looks at her hand. Ariana can tell that she sees Sibley.

Gwendolyn's face changes. The tears have stopped. Her jaw is set. There's a glint in her eye. There is a light around her.

Together, holding Sibley, Gwendolyn and Ariana lift their hands to the sky, being careful not to look at the Jagwa.

The demons surround Lochlan, Asher, and Larque.

A beam of white light pours out from Ariana and Gwendolyn's hands.

It is different than the beam that radiated from Asher and Ariana. This one sparkles and twinkles in the night. It is beautiful.

Elora's form begins to shrink.

"Noooo!" she screams. "What twins have defeated me?" she demands as she grows smaller against the colours moving slowly across the sky. "I have the boy! The girl is below!"

The Jagwa demons hiss, then fall silent and disappear.

Lochlan, Asher, and Larque fall from the grip of the black cloud. They hit the earth with three loud thuds.

"Noooooo!" shrieks Elora. "I will come back to this place. You will never be free from me..."

The witch Elora, reduced to a speck of white light, glimmers briefly in the sky like a star, before fading to nothing.

Exhausted, Ariana falls to the ground. Sibley whispers in Gwendolyn's ear. "Well done, Sister," she says. "Well done."

CHAPTER TWENTY-FOUR

Rain

WHEN LOCHLAN and Gwendolyn return home with Larque and the twins, the skies open and rain spills upon the land. The entire kingdom must be cleansed after all that has happened.

Inside, Gwendolyn listens to the raindrops splash upon the earth outside the hut. The sound is almost deafening, but Ariana and Asher are sleeping soundly on the mat in the corner. This is all Gwendolyn has ever wanted. To have her children safe here. Together. Where they belong. *Where has he been all these years?* she thinks. It breaks Gwendolyn's heart to think about it, but the important thing is he is back.

After a few moments, the raindrops slow to a gentle tapping rhythm on the rocks of the hut.

Gwendolyn is soothed by the sound of the rain while she watches her children sleep.

She is lost in thought.

The memories flood back to her, of her and Sibley.

When I was a little girl, she was always there, she thinks.

Gwendolyn remembers believing Sibley was her sister. And that was what she whispered to her this evening before she disappeared again. *Sister.*

Gwendolyn pulls a wool blanket around her shoulders. Lochlan and Larque face each other at the kitchen table.

"Are either of you hungry?" Gwendolyn asks. "I can make breakfast."

She receives no reply.

Lochlan speaks for the first time since they got home. "You owe us an explanation, Larque," he says.

Gwendolyn stokes the fire and puts four sausages in the pan with some butter as Lochlan waits for Larque to speak.

Larque removes his hood.

"Your face!" Gwendolyn exclaims.

Larque touches his face, which is now smooth and unblemished.

"Elora. She's been destroyed. The effects of her powers must have come undone," he says, smiling.

"I was in love with her," Larque begins. "We were very young when we met. No older than Asher and Ariana are now. She was as sweet and charming as she was beautiful. At least that's how it appeared in the beginning."

Gwendolyn sets a plate of biscuits and mugs of hot tea in front of Lochlan and Larque before cracking three eggs into the pan. They land with a sizzle.

"Eventually we married and had a set of twins and two more children after that. We were so happy. She was a wonderful wife and mother. But as the children grew older, Elora changed." A tortured look comes over his face.

"As I would later discover, she had only wanted children so she could use them for her spells. She knew I was a wizard and the son of a pure heart and she sought me out because of these things. She bewitched our twins for her own protection. Made it so that they would have the power to save her if someone ever tried to destroy her."

Gwendolyn puts a plate of sausages and eggs on the table, but they sit untouched as none of the three feels like eating.

"So," Lochlan says to Larque, "You're the father of Elora's children." Lochlan pauses. "That makes you my own distant grandfather doesn't it?"

"Yes," Larque confirms.

Gwendolyn listens to the soft breathing of Ariana and Asher. Of the raindrops tapping the stones.

"What kind of spells was Elora using?" Gwendolyn asks.

"She thought she could manipulate me into joining her in her evil plan, to see what the world could be like if ruled by maleficent hands. She needed the blood of children for her plan to work. Elora had intended to kill our other two children, to harvest their hearts at different ages, so she could determine when a child's innocence would be most potent for her spells."

Gwendolyn's stomach sinks. But there is more. He keeps talking.

"She had a grand scheme to collect all children under the age of thirteen to harvest their hearts for her experiments. She planned to kill me, too, since she'd had the children she needed. She had no use for me. And she knew I would stop her."

Lochlan turns pale. *My relative—the good witch Elora—was a monster.*

"What did you do?" Gwendolyn asks.

"I consulted the Book Of Whispers and learned about Elora's plans to release the Jagwa demons. If she did this, she could quickly get rid of all humans. The human heart stops beating at the sight of a fully formed Jagwa."

"Why did she want to get rid of all humans?" Lochlan asks, finding his voice again.

"With humans gone, Elora planned to produce a super race of dark sorcerers and witches like an evil science project," Larque explains. "According to prophecy, it was only twins who could release her."

"What about her twin? What happened to her?" Gwendolyn asks.

"The legend states that Calla died mysteriously," says Larque.

"Yes," says Lochlan. "We know. Elora's grief caused a curse to spread across the land."

"No, that is not the truth," explains Larque. "Calla did not die, but she did disappear. And Elora certainly did not grieve her loss."

He pauses, sips his tea.

"Can you tell us more about Calla?" Lochlan asks.

"In time," Larque replies.

"Larque, what happened to your children?" Gwendolyn asks.

"Elora had threatened to kill our children, and I was not going to let that happen," Larque says. "I was not powerful enough to destroy her, because she is immortal. But I managed to encase her in stone. I knew I then must separate our twins so that they would not be able to release their evil mother into the world again. It was the most difficult decision I have ever had to make, but I knew it needed to be done. While I was turning her to stone, she put a spell on me, casting me out into an invisible prison. I couldn't warn anyone."

Larque's face falls at the thought of his children.

"Larque," Lochlan starts, "are you also immortal?"

"Yes," says Larque. "Though that never stopped Elora from trying to kill me. There are always ways to destroy an immortal, but you must find their unique weakness."

Gwendolyn looks at Larque and says, "If you were banished, how did you separate your children?"

"The goblin Grimblerod agreed to take my children

and separate them, protecting the world from Elora. To be sure that Elora would stay in her stone form, I had Grimblerod separate every set of twins born in Valorium, Rhyme, the kingdom of Falmoor, and throughout surrounding kingdoms. It was the only way to ensure that she could not be released to carry out her evil plans."

Gwendolyn notices the rain has stopped. It is starting to grow lighter. She gazes at the twins and sees they are still sleeping. She reaches to the plate of biscuits sitting on the table and takes one. She mindlessly picks crumbs off of it and puts them in her mouth.

"Elora was such a powerful force, she retained the ability to speak to her descendants even from the realm she was in all those years," Larque continues. "She lured you to Rhyme because she wanted your twins. With Gwendolyn's pure heart and your magic blood, she knew your heirs would be extremely powerful."

Gwendolyn pours more tea in the three mugs.

"I couldn't risk them getting to her," Larque says, looking at Gwendolyn. "You were tricked into coming to Rhyme because having you closer to her would give her more power over you."

"Where has Asher been all this time?" Gwendolyn asks.

"He was to be taken to the same place as the others. But Grimblerod wanted Asher for himself. Because he was older than the babies he had been taking, he wanted to use him to work in his underground tunnels. I forbade this, yet Grimblerod threatened to lure Ariana and bring the twins together if I stopped him. I attempted to use magic to manipulate him, but my powers were useless with him living beneath the pixie tree where he was protected by its enchantment."

Larque looks down at the table.

"If only I knew twins would also have the power to destroy her…" His voice trails off.

"Are you telling us," says Lochlan, "that our boy has been kept underground for eight years?"

"Yes," confirms Larque.

Lochlan puts his head in his hands.

"Larque," Gwendolyn asks, with tears in her eyes,

"what happened to your children? What happened to all of those children?"

Larque takes a deep breath and exhales. "I will show you."

CHAPTER TWENTY-FIVE

The Voice

GRIMBLEROD RETURNS to his cave with the rising sun that morning with a breakfast of field mice, wild mushrooms, and crickets for the boy. But when he pushes back the insect wing curtain to Asher's room, the boy is not there.

His candle is present but the flame no longer flickers. Globs of cold wax are piled around the brass candle holder.

His fat green feet carry Grimblerod through the small wooden door of his home, through the extensive series of tunnels that make up the underground lair. Most of them were dug by Asher over the years.

Grimblerod sniffs and sniffs but he can't detect human. This is unusual because the boy always stinks.

Grimblerod grunts as he runs with a torch in hand, searching every tunnel. He waddles to his secret cave, the place where he keeps his trinkets. The door to this cave is made to look like dirt so it blends in with the rest of the tunnel. He digs through the pile until he pulls out a bright blue gem. The boy's voice. It's still there.

He will be back.

CHAPTER TWENTY-SIX

Bonus: First Chapter of Into Coraira

SHIVERING, ASGALL instinctively rubs his hands together for warmth.

His breath hangs in clouds in the early morning air, the only sign that someone—or something—lurks among the rubble of Elora's fallen statue.

It is colder here than he remembers. Had he known last night that Bardrick planned to open the portal to Darali for the first time in centuries, he would have been more prepared. As it was, he'd been forced to make a quick, quiet escape.

Once the most powerful sorcerer in the universe,

Asgall is weak in this form. He must feed on something soon to gain strength so he can start doing his work or he will die.

And he can't feed until he finds a suitable host.

What was that?

A zap of energy—a burst of air—whizzes past.

Asgall watches a flash of light appear in front of him before it drops to the ground where his feet should be.

Fairies? I haven't seen one of those little nuisances in hundreds of years.

Asgall watches two fairies explore the pile of grey rocks, neither of the two much bigger than a humming bird. Both fairies have butterfly-shaped wings, iridescent like dragonflies. The female's wings twinkle blue, matching her hair, which is tied back out of her face. The male is not nearly as brightly coloured as the female. His wings also twinkle, but his hair is a dull brown and he has no unusual features to speak of, but for a spattering of freckles across the bridge of his nose.

The fairies are unaware of the mist that watches them.

I can't believe that useless race survived.

"Thank goodness the heavy rain has stopped," says the female fairy to her companion. She effortlessly flips over a piece of rock the size of a loaf of bread.

I'd forgotten how strong these creatures can be.

She lands with a splash in a puddle, covering her with dirty water.

What could they be looking for?

"This would be much easier at mid-day," grunts the male fairy as he pushes a fragment of stone out of his way. "It's still dark!"

"Humans can't see us, but they might wonder how all the rocks are moving around on their own!" the female says. She flies to her left, then to her right. "She said it would be here somewhere—"

"Oh! Look, Sibley! I think that might be it!" The male flies to a spot past the pile of stones.

The female, apparently named Sibley, flies to join her

friend, where he stands over a pendant almost the size of his small body.

"Yes, Cinnamon!" she says, leaning down and running her hands over the smooth surface of the pendant. "See, there are three small fissures just below, where the crystals were fused back together."

Hmmm, what is this? Asgall drifts closer to the fairies to see what they're looking at.

"We better get this back to Calla," Cinnamon exclaims, wrapping the long gold chain around his waist. He picks up one end of the crystal and gestures for Sibley to do the same.

One of these creatures might make a suitable host, Asgall thinks. *They're rather small but they're strong—wait, that name he just said—did he say "Calla"?*

"I've got it!" says Sibley, holding her end of the pendant with both hands.

"Hurry, it's starting to rain again!" shouts Cinnamon as fat raindrops fall from the sky.

I must get to Calla. I must find out what the fairies know.

But before Asgall can inhabit one of the fairies' bodies, they dart off to the pixie tree as the pale morning sun peeks over the horizon into a dark grey sky.

I have missed my chance.

In the wet grass just beyond the pile of grey rock, a fat robin plucks a reluctant worm from the earth.

That will do, thinks Asgall, watching the worm disappear down the robin's yellow beak. *That will do fine.*

Asgall drifts closer to the robin.

And just like that, Asgall is mist no more.

Copyright Info

First Printing December 2014

Acknowledgements

As I sit here writing the acknowledgements page for my first novel, there are tears in my eyes and a smile on my face. Writing this page makes it all real.

For as long as I can remember, I've dreamed of being an author. I have written numerous books over the years as a ghostwriter, but this novel marks the first instance in which my name is printed on the cover.

Funny, though, that in my dreams, writing a book was not nearly so much work. There have been many people involved to help make this dream come true.

Hugh. (a.k.a. Mr. MacDonald). As an insecure teenager, there was only one thing I felt confident about —that I could write a story. Thank you for reinforcing that, and for encouraging me to never stop writing. I never learned more from a teacher than I did from you.

Heidi. You have given me a tremendous gift. How can I ever thank you for making my dreams come true? I can't wait to see what the Universe has in store for us next.

Chris. I sent you my first draft and a second draft and a third draft (and a fourth draft and a fifth) of a good story. And thanks to your tremendous talent, we have created a beautiful piece of literature from that first rough cut. Your talent continues to amaze me. Thank you for helping my words to twinkle, and thank you for being there always.

Sarah. The artwork is perfect. There is nothing more to say. But I hope we can continue to do this when you're a world-famous artist.

Cam and Austin, you will never know how much I appreciate you reading this book and for telling me how to make it better.

Sierra, thank you for your eyes on the early version of this book and for giving me your valuable input.

Dad, thank you for teaching me how to make up stories. Mom, thank you for teaching me how to put them into words. Krystal, for taking the time to read the drafts and for being one of my biggest cheerleaders. Chance and BJ, you guys are awesome, too. Keep the honest feedback coming.

Jason. If it was not for your blind trust in me and your unwavering support, I would most likely be a miserable soul wondering what might have been had I taken that leap when my heart told me to. Thank you for believing in me. And thank you for all of the ideas and inspiration you planted in my head that helped to make Ariana and Asher's story so interesting. This story would not be nearly as rich without your creative input. I love you.

Casey and Shelby, thank you for never getting sick of hearing the story. I hope you will always want to read what I write.

Discussion Questions

How do you think Asher felt on his first night asleep in Grimblerod's Underground Lair?

Do you think Grimblerod felt any remorse about taking the twins for Larque?

Do you believe there's any significance to all of the pebbles that Larque has kept over the years?

Where do you think the missing twins went?

What do you think happened to Elora's twin sister, Calla?

What was the relationship like between Sibley and Gwendolyn? How did it change?

Do you think Gwendolyn and Lochlan made a good decision when they moved to Rhyme?

Why do you think Novah has lived to such an old age? Do you think the island really is magic, or do you think it's just her?

Do you think Asher will get his voice back? How do you imagine that might happen?

Do you think we'll see Elora again?

About Jaime Lee Mann

Jaime Lee Mann was born and raised in a sweet little house by the sea in Prince Edward Island. The eldest of four, Jaime Lee and her sister could be found any day of the week playing make-believe on the rocky shore below their home, or in their own personal magic forest. (Their younger brothers weren't allowed to follow them.)

Jaime Lee was drawn to books at a very young age and always had one on the go. She decided as a child that she would write books of her own when she grew up. As she got older, Jaime Lee would bring her notebook and pencil to the beach or the woods and write her stories and poetry there. (To this day, her muse finds her in such places.)

The salty air of her childhood home has provided a wealth of inspiration for Jaime Lee's creative writing throughout her life, and she often finds herself drawn there today. Her second novel was outlined on the same rocks she played on as a child, right below her parents' house.

As Jaime Lee grew older, her desire to write never

went away, but it took a back seat as she struggled to choose the right career path. She spent time at university studying English and at college, learning about entrepreneurship. As a new mother, with her husband Jason's support, she decided to stay home to care for their children. This allowed Jaime Lee to start her own business called Mann Made Time, where she worked as a virtual assistant.

Her business did very well and two years after their first baby was born, Jaime Lee and Jason welcomed a second little girl into their family. It was around this time that Jaime Lee transitioned her business to solely provide the type of services she most enjoyed — copywriting and ghostwriting. She called her business Mann Made Copy and was happy to finally have an opportunity to write full-time.

Years later, that business would evolve into a partnership called Manley Mann Media, which Jaime Lee formed with a professional editor by the name of Christine Gordon Manley.

Over the years, Jaime Lee has written about many topics including interior design, ant bait, meal-planning, gluten, computer software, and Disney World. She has also ghostwritten manuscripts for all types of people with many different stories, and some of those manuscripts have gone on to become published works.

In 2014, Jaime Lee decided to dust off her dream of publishing her own works. She submitted her children's picture book, A bug is a bug is a bug, for publication with Toronto publishing company Blue Moon Publishers. The manuscript was well received, and that title is expected to be published in the summer of 2015. In the meantime, Blue Moon Publishers has also opted to publish a series of middle grade fiction novels Jaime Lee dreamed up while telling bedtime stories to her daughters. The first book in the Legend of Rhyme series, Elora of Stone, is the first novel to be published with Jaime Lee's own name on the cover.

When Jaime Lee isn't writing (for herself or someone else), she can most likely be found playing Barbie with her daughters, working out at the local kettlebell studio, or in the kitchen making something delicious.

Jaime is currently working on the next instalment in the Legend of Rhyme series. You can read more on her site:

jaimeleemann.com
or connect with her on:
Twitter: twitter.com/jaimeleemann

Facebook: facebook.com/JaimeMann
Pinterest: pinterest.com/jaimeleemann/
Goodreads: goodreads.com/user/show/34635028-jaime-lee-mann
Instagram: instagram.com/jaimeleemann

Jaime greatly appreciates you taking the time to read this work. Please consider leaving a review wherever you bought the book, or telling your friends or blog readers about the Legend of Rhyme series, to help spread the word. Thank you for your support.

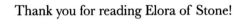
Thank you for reading Elora of Stone!

CPSIA information can be obtained at www.ICGtesting.com
Printed in the USA
LVOW10s1717141016

508828LV00017B/221/P